DOVER · THRIFT · EDITIONS

R. U. R.
(Rossum's Universal Robots)

KAREL ČAPEK

Translated by

PAUL SELVER and NIGEL PLAYFAIR

DOVER PUBLICATIONS, INC.
Mineola, New York

DOVER THRIFT EDITIONS

GENERAL EDITOR: PAUL NEGRI
EDITOR OF THIS VOLUME: DREW SILVER

Bibliographical Note

This Dover edition, first published in 2001, is an unabridged republication of the text of the Theater Guild English-language version first published by Doubleday, Page & Company, Garden City, New York in 1923.

Library of Congress Cataloging-in-Publication Data

Čapek, Karel, 1890–1938.
 [R.U.R. English]
 R.U.R. (Rossum's universal robots) / Karel Čapek ; translated by Paul Selver and Nigel Playfair.
  p. cm. — (Dover thrift editions)
 Originally published: Garden City, N.Y. : Doubleday, Page, 1923. (Theatre Guild library).
 ISBN 0-486-41926-6 (pbk.)
  I. Title: Rossum's universal robots. II. Selver, Paul, 1888– III. Playfair, Nigel, Sir, 1874–1934. IV. Title.

PG5038.C3 R213 2001
891.8'6252—dc21

2001028651

Manufactured in the United States of America
Dover Publications, Inc., 31 East 2nd Street, Mineola, N.Y. 11501

Note

KAREL ČAPEK (1890–1938) was one of the best-known literary figures of independent Czechoslovakia between the two world wars. A satirist and a politically engaged philosopher, he was a journalist and editor, a theater manager and producer, an essayist, a travel writer, a prolific novelist and a highly successful playwright.

Čapek's literary work dealt with questions of moral philosophy and human values. His fiction and theater work was often cast in the form of science-fiction romance. *The Insect Play* (1921), an international hit, was an allegory of human beastliness with insects as stand-ins for people. The novel *Krakatit* (1924) concerned an explosive with the potential to destroy civilization. *The War With the Newts* (1936), probably Čapek's best-known work of fiction, sought to represent the state of the world in the 1930s, investigating science, international politics and social ethics through the story of the discovery and exploitation of a population of intelligent salamanders by multinational capitalists, and the consequences in economic depression, political revolt and war. Other works, especially a trilogy of philosophical novels (*Hordubal*, 1933; *Meteor*, 1934; *An Ordinary Life*, 1934), considered moral questions and the nature of reality in less satirical and fantastic terms. In his essays and newspaper columns, Čapek examined the character of social institutions and promoted a liberal, democratic politics and social ethics. A thinker who always sought a moderate position based on respect and sympathy for others' beliefs and motives (a selection of his work published in 1990 was entitled *Toward the Radical Center*), he was a close friend, political supporter and biographer of Tomas G. Masaryk. Like many humane Europeans, he was appalled by the bloody brutality of World War I and the moral obtuseness of the political order that produced it, and tended toward pacifism in the years afterward. But as the political situation in the 1930s, and in particular the prospects for his own country, worsened beyond the capacity of satire to address, he became an increasingly outspoken antifascist and ultimately endorsed armed resistance to tyranny. It is said that he would have been awarded the Nobel Prize for literature in those years, had not the Nobel committee been fearful of offending Hitler.

R.U.R. (Rossum's Universal Robots) is undoubtedly Čapek's best-known work in the English-speaking world. Written in 1920, it was, like *The Insect Play*, an international hit (the Theatre Guild production appeared on Broadway in 1922). Remembered for introducing the word "robot" (the term, suggested by Josef Čapek, derives from a Czech dialect word for "drudgery"), *R.U.R.* is a fantasy on the unintended consequences of technological *hubris*. This is a theme that was in the air in the years after World War I. (Some might feel that it warrants further consideration.)

The robots in *R.U.R.* are built to labor. They do it so well that, as one character points out, the prices of agricultural and manufactured goods have dropped almost to nothing; as another points out, millions are out of work, too. Trouble is building, but the robot business is too profitable for the manufacturers to consider stopping, no matter what the consequences, and rationalizations are always at hand. And these problems are soon overshadowed by another: the robots have acquired souls and are rising up against their rulers, the humans. *Things*, literally, are out of control.

Despite its darkness, the play seems to shy away from the harshest implications of its own premises—humans are wiped out by the robots, and yet somehow, in the end, the robots become human. Love and laughter and the dignity of work are endorsed, and the survival of humanity is assured. In the words of Rene Wellek, there is a "sleight of hand" that sentimentally undercuts the point of the story. Perhaps in 1920, even after a senseless and catastrophic war, it was too hard for Čapek to take the implications completely seriously; perhaps the creation—as a result of that very war—of the liberal, democratic Czechoslovakia to which he was so passionately committed, allowed him to remain optimistic. Or perhaps hopeless pessimism would just have made bad theater. Critics who have commented on Čapek's plays have all praised his dramatic stagecraft, and *R.U.R.*'s lumbering automatons and ominous suggestions of impending violence clearly make for effective melodrama. Nevertheless, as Wellek says, *R.U.R.*'s "warning of mankind against the dangers of machine civilization, seemed very healthy."

Karel Čapek died of pneumonia on Christmas day, 1938, not long after Munich; he is said to have lost the will to live after his country's death sentence. His older brother Josef—an artist and writer, and Karel's frequent collaborator earlier in their careers—was perhaps not so lucky. Also a prominent liberal and antifascist, he was arrested by the Germans shortly after the invasion in 1939 and died at the Belsen concentration camp in April 1945.

Characters

HARRY DOMIN—*General Manager of Rossum's Universal Robots.*
SULLA—*A Robotess.*
MARIUS—*A Robot.*
HELENA GLORY.
DR. GALL—*Head of the Physiological and Experimental Department of R. U. R.*
MR. FABRY—*Engineer General, Technical Controller of R. U. R.*
DR. HALLEMEIER—*Head of the Institute for Psychological Training of Robots.*
MR. ALQUIST—*Architect, Head of the Works Department of R. U. R.*
CONSUL BUSMAN—*General Business Manager of R. U. R.*
NANA.
RADIUS—*A Robot.*
HELENA—*A Robotess.*
PRIMUS—*A Robot.*
A SERVANT.
FIRST ROBOT.
SECOND ROBOT.
THIRD ROBOT.

ACT I
Central Office of the Factory of Rossum's Universal Robots.

ACT II
Helena's Drawing Room—Ten years later. Morning.

ACT III
The Same Afternoon

EPILOGUE
A Laboratory—One year later.

Place: An Island.   *Time: The Future.*

ACT I

[*Central office of the factory of Rossum's Universal Robots.
Entrance on the right. The windows on the front wall look out on the
rows of factory chimneys. On the left more managing departments.*
DOMIN *is sitting in the revolving chair at a large American writing table.
On the left-hand wall large maps showing steamship and railroad routes.
On the right-hand wall are fastened printed placards. ("Robot's
Cheapest Labor," etc.) In contrast to these wall fittings, the floor is cov-
ered with a splendid Turkish carpet, a sofa, leather armchair, and filing
cabinets. At a desk near the windows* SULLA *is typing letters.*]

DOMIN [*Dictating*] Ready?
SULLA Yes.
DOMIN To E. M. McVicker and Co., Southampton, England. "We
undertake no guarantee for goods damaged in transit. As soon as
the consignment was taken on board we drew your captain's at-
tention to the fact that the vessel was unsuitable for the transport
of Robots, and we are therefore not responsible for spoiled freight.
We beg to remain for Rossum's Universal Robots. Yours truly."
[SULLA, *who has sat motionless during dictation, now types rapidly
for a few seconds, then stops, withdrawing the completed letter.*]
Ready?
SULLA Yes.
DOMIN Another letter. To the E. B. Huyson Agency, New York,
U.S.A. "We beg to acknowledge receipt of order for five thousand
Robots. As you are sending your own vessel, please dispatch as
cargo equal quantities of soft and hard coal for R.U.R., the same
to be credited as part payment of the amount due to us. We beg to
remain, for Rossum's Universal Robots. Yours truly." [SULLA *re-
peats the rapid typing.*] Ready?
SULLA Yes.
DOMIN Another letter. "Friedrichswerks, Hamburg, Germany. We
beg to acknowledge receipt of order for fifteen thousand Robots."
[*Telephone rings.*] Hello! This is the Central Office. Yes.

1

Certainly. Well, send them a wire. Good. [*Hangs up telephone.*] Where did I leave off?

SULLA "We beg to acknowledge receipt of order for fifteen thousand Robots."

DOMIN Fifteen thousand R. Fifteen thousand R.

[*Enter* MARIUS.]

DOMIN Well, what is it?

MARIUS There's a lady, sir, asking to see you.

DOMIN A lady? Who is she?

MARIUS I don't know, sir. She brings this card of introduction.

DOMIN [*Reads the card*] Ah, from President Glory. Ask her to come in.

MARIUS Please step this way.

[*Enter* HELENA GLORY.]
[*Exit* MARIUS.]

HELENA How do you do?

DOMIN How do you do. [*Standing up.*] What can I do for you?

HELENA You are Mr. Domin, the General Manager.

DOMIN I am.

HELENA I have come——

DOMIN With President Glory's card. That is quite sufficient.

HELENA President Glory is my father. I am Helena Glory.

DOMIN Miss Glory, this is such a great honor for us to be allowed to welcome our great President's daughter, that——

HELENA That you can't show me the door?

DOMIN Please sit down. Sulla, you may go.

[*Exit* SULLA.]

[*Sitting down.*] How can I be of service to you, Miss Glory?

HELENA I have come——

DOMIN To have a look at our famous works where people are manufactured. Like all visitors. Well, there is no objection.

HELENA I thought it was forbidden to——

DOMIN To enter the factory. Yes, of course. Everybody comes here with someone's visiting card, Miss Glory.

HELENA And you show them——

DOMIN Only certain things. The manufacture of artificial people is a secret process.

HELENA If you only knew how enormously that——

DOMIN Interests me. Europe's talking about nothing else.

HELENA Why don't you let me finish speaking?

DOMIN   I beg your pardon. Did you want to say something different?

HELENA   I only wanted to ask——

DOMIN   Whether I could make a special exception in your case and show you our factory. Why, certainly Miss Glory.

HELENA   How do you know I wanted to say that?

DOMIN   They all do. But we shall consider it a special honor to show you more than we do the rest.

HELENA   Thank you.

DOMIN   But you must agree not to divulge the least . . .

HELENA   [Standing up and giving him her hand] My word of honor.

DOMIN   Thank you. Won't you raise your veil?

HELENA   Of course. You want to see whether I'm a spy or not. I beg your pardon.

DOMIN   What is it?

HELENA   Would you mind releasing my hand?

DOMIN   [Releasing it] I beg your pardon.

HELENA   [Raising her veil] How cautious you have to be here, don't you?

DOMIN   [Observing her with deep interest] Hm, of course—we—that is——

HELENA   But what is it? What's the matter?

DOMIN   I'm remarkably pleased. Did you have a pleasant crossing?

HELENA   Yes.

DOMIN   No difficulty?

HELENA   Why?

DOMIN   What I mean to say is—you're so young.

HELENA   May we go straight into the factory?

DOMIN   Yes. Twenty-two, I think.

HELENA   Twenty-two what?

DOMIN   Years.

HELENA   Twenty-one. Why do you want to know?

DOMIN   Because—as— [with enthusiasm] you will make a long stay, won't you?

HELENA   That depends on how much of the factory you show me.

DOMIN   Oh, hang the factory. Oh, no, no, you shall see everything, Miss Glory. Indeed you shall. Won't you sit down?

HELENA   [Crossing to couch and sitting] Thank you.

DOMIN   But first would you like to hear the story of the invention?

HELENA   Yes, indeed.

DOMIN   [Observes HELENA with rapture and reels off rapidly] It was in the year 1920 that old Rossum, the great physiologist, who was then quite a young scientist, took himself to this distant island for the purpose of studying the ocean fauna, full stop. On this occasion he attempted by chemical synthesis to imitate the living matter known as protoplasm until he suddenly discovered a substance which behaved exactly like living matter although its chemical composition was different. That was in the year of 1932, exactly four hundred forty years after the discovery of America. Whew!

HELENA Do you know that by heart?

DOMIN Yes. You see physiology is not in my line. Shall I go on?

HELENA Yes, please.

DOMIN And then, Miss Glory, old Rossum wrote the following among his chemical specimens: "Nature has found only one method of organizing living matter. There is, however, another method, more simple, flexible and rapid, which has not yet occurred to nature at all. This second process by which life can be developed was discovered by me to-day." Now imagine him, Miss Glory, writing those wonderful words over some colloidal mess that a dog wouldn't look at. Imagine him sitting over a test tube, and thinking how the whole tree of life would grow from it, how all animals would proceed from it, beginning with some sort of beetle and ending with a man. A man of different substance from us. Miss Glory, that was a tremendous moment.

HELENA Well?

DOMIN Now, the thing was how to get the life out of the test tubes, and hasten development and form organs, bones and nerves, and so on, and find such substances as catalytics, enzymes, hormones, and so forth, in short—you understand?

HELENA Not much, I'm afraid.

DOMIN Never mind. You see with the help of his tinctures he could make whatever he wanted. He could have produced a Medusa with the brain of a Socrates or a worm fifty yards long. But being without a grain of humor, he took it into his head to make a vertebrate or perhaps a man. This artificial living matter of his had a raging thirst for life. It didn't mind being sewn or mixed together. That couldn't be done with natural albumen. And that's how he set about it.

HELENA About what?

DOMIN About imitating nature. First of all he tried making an artificial dog. That took him several years and resulted in a sort of stunted calf which died in a few days. I'll show it to you in the museum. And then old Rossum started on the manufacture of man.

HELENA And I must divulge this to nobody?

DOMIN To nobody in the world.

HELENA What a pity that it's to be found in all the school books of both Europe and America.

DOMIN   Yes. But do you know what isn't in the school books? That old Rossum was mad. Seriously, Miss Glory, you must keep this to yourself. The old crank wanted to actually make people.

HELENA   But you do make people.

DOMIN   Approximately, Miss Glory. But old Rossum meant it literally. He wanted to become a sort of scientific substitute for God. He was a fearful materialist, and that's why he did it all. His sole purpose was nothing more nor less than to prove that God was no longer necessary. Do you know anything about anatomy?

HELENA   Very little.

DOMIN   Neither do I. Well, he then decided to manufacture everything as in the human body. I'll show you in the museum the bungling attempt it took him ten years to produce. It was to have been a man, but it lived for three days only. Then up came young Rossum, an engineer. He was a wonderful fellow, Miss Glory. When he saw what a mess of it the old man was making, he said: "It's absurd to spend ten years making a man. If you can't make him quicker than nature, you might as well shut up shop." Then he set about learning anatomy himself.

HELENA   There's nothing about that in the school books.

DOMIN   No. The school books are full of paid advertisements, and rubbish at that. What the school books say about the united efforts of the two great Rossums is all a fairy tale. They used to have dreadful rows. The old atheist hadn't the slightest conception of industrial matters, and the end of it was that young Rossum shut him up in some laboratory or other and let him fritter the time away with his monstrosities, while he himself started on the business from an engineer's point of view. Old Rossum cursed him and before he died he managed to botch up two physiological horrors. Then one day they found him dead in the laboratory. And that's his whole story.

HELENA   And what about the young man?

DOMIN   Well, any one who has looked into human anatomy will have seen at once that man is too complicated, and that a good engineer could make him more simply. So young Rossum began to overhaul anatomy and tried to see what could be left out or simplified. In short—but this isn't boring you, Miss Glory?

HELENA   No indeed. You're—it's awfully interesting.

DOMIN   So young Rossum said to himself: "A man is something that feels happy, plays the piano, likes going for a walk, and in fact, wants to do a whole lot of things that are really unnecessary."

HELENA   Oh.

DOMIN That are unnecessary when he wants, let us say, to weave or count. Do you play the piano?

HELENA Yes.

DOMIN That's good. But a working machine must not play the piano, must not feel happy, must not do a whole lot of other things. A gasoline motor must not have tassels or ornaments, Miss Glory. And to manufacture artificial workers is the same thing as to manufacture gasoline motors. The process must be of the simplest, and the product of the best from a practical point of view. What sort of worker do you think is the best from a practical point of view?

HELENA What?

DOMIN What sort of worker do you think is the best from a practical point of view?

HELENA Perhaps the one who is most honest and hardworking.

DOMIN No; the one that is the cheapest. The one whose requirements are the smallest. Young Rossum invented a worker with the minimum amount of requirements. He had to simplify him. He rejected everything that did not contribute directly to the progress of work—everything that makes man more expensive. In fact, he rejected man and made the Robot. My dear Miss Glory, the Robots are not people. Mechanically they are more perfect than we are, they have an enormously developed intelligence, but they have no soul.

HELENA How do you know they've no soul?

DOMIN Have you ever seen what a Robot looks like inside?

HELENA No.

DOMIN Very neat, very simple. Really, a beautiful piece of work. Not much in it, but everything in flawless order. The product of an engineer is technically at a higher pitch of perfection than a product of nature.

HELENA But man is supposed to be the product of God.

DOMIN All the worse. God hasn't the least notion of modern engineering. Would you believe that young Rossum then proceeded to play at being God?

HELENA How do you mean?

DOMIN He began to manufacture Super-Robots. Regular giants they were. He tried to make them twelve feet tall. But you wouldn't believe what a failure they were.

HELENA A failure?

DOMIN Yes. For no reason at all their limbs used to keep snapping off. Evidently our planet is too small for giants. Now we only make Robots of normal size and of very high class human finish.

HELENA   I saw the first Robots at home. The town counsel bought
    them for—I mean engaged them for work.
DOMIN   Bought them, dear Miss Glory. Robots are bought and sold.
HELENA   These were employed as street sweepers. I saw them sweep-
    ing. They were so strange and quiet.
DOMIN   Rossum's Universal Robot factory doesn't produce a uniform
    brand of Robots. We have Robots of finer and coarser grades. The
    best will live about twenty years. [*He rings for* MARIUS.]
HELENA   Then they die?
DOMIN   Yes, they get used up.

[*Enter* MARIUS.]

DOMIN   Marius, bring in samples of the Manual Labor Robot.

[*Exit* MARIUS.]

DOMIN   I'll show you specimens of the two extremes. This first grade
    is comparatively inexpensive and is made in vast quantities.

[MARIUS *reenters with two Manual Labor Robots.*]

DOMIN   There you are; as powerful as a small tractor. Guaranteed to
    have average intelligence. That will do, Marius.

[MARIUS *exits with Robots.*]

HELENA   They make me feel so strange.
DOMIN   [*Rings*] Did you see my new typist? [*He rings for* SULLA.]
HELENA   I didn't notice her.

[*Enter* SULLA.]

DOMIN   Sulla, let Miss Glory see you.
HELENA   So pleased to meet you. You must find it terribly dull in this
    out-of-the-way spot, don't you?
SULLA   I don't know, Miss Glory.
HELENA   Where do you come from?
SULLA   From the factory.
HELENA   Oh, you were born there?
SULLA   I was made there.
HELENA   What?
DOMIN   [*Laughing*] Sulla is a Robot, best grade.
HELENA   Oh, I beg your pardon.
DOMIN   Sulla isn't angry. See, Miss Glory, the kind of skin we make.
    [*Feels the skin on* SULLA's *face.*] Feel her face.
HELENA   Oh, no, no.

DOMIN   You wouldn't know that she's made of different material from us, would you? Turn round, Sulla.

HELENA   Oh, stop, stop.

DOMIN   Talk to Miss Glory, Sulla.

SULLA   Please sit down. [HELENA *sits.*] Did you have a pleasant crossing?

HELENA   Oh, yes, certainly.

SULLA   Don't go back on the *Amelia*, Miss Glory. The barometer is falling steadily. Wait for the *Pennsylvania*. That's a good, powerful vessel.

DOMIN   What's its speed?

SULLA   Twenty knots. Fifty thousand tons. One of the latest vessels, Miss Glory.

HELENA   Thank you.

SULLA   A crew of fifteen hundred, Captain Harpy, eight boilers——

DOMIN   That'll do, Sulla. Now show us your knowledge of French.

HELENA   You know French?

SULLA   I know four languages. I can write: Dear Sir, Monsieur, Geehrter Herr, Cteny pane.

HELENA   [*Jumping up*] Oh, that's absurd! Sulla isn't a Robot. Sulla is a girl like me. Sulla, this is outrageous! Why do you take part in such a hoax?

SULLA   I am a Robot.

HELENA   No, no, you are not telling the truth. I know they've forced you to do it for an advertisement. Sulla, you are a girl like me, aren't you?

DOMIN   I'm sorry, Miss Glory. Sulla is a Robot.

HELENA   It's a lie!

DOMIN   What? [*Rings.*] Excuse me, Miss Glory, then I must convince you.

[*Enter* MARIUS.]

DOMIN   Marius, take Sulla into the dissecting room, and tell them to open her up at once.

HELENA   Where?

DOMIN   Into the dissecting room. When they've cut her open, you can go and have a look.

HELENA   No, no!

DOMIN   Excuse me, you spoke of lies.

HELENA   You wouldn't have her killed?

DOMIN   You can't kill machines.

HELENA   Don't be afraid, Sulla, I won't let you go. Tell me, my dear,

are they always so cruel to you? You mustn't put up with it, Sulla.
You mustn't.

SULLA   I am a Robot.

HELENA   That doesn't matter. Robots are just as good as we are. Sulla,
you wouldn't let yourself be cut to pieces?

SULLA   Yes.

HELENA   Oh, you're not afraid of death, then?

SULLA   I cannot tell, Miss Glory.

HELENA   Do you know what would happen to you in there?

SULLA   Yes, I should cease to move.

HELENA   How dreadful!

DOMIN   Marius, tell Miss Glory what you are.

MARIUS   Marius, the Robot.

DOMIN   Would you take Sulla into the dissecting room?

MARIUS   Yes.

DOMIN   Would you be sorry for her?

MARIUS   I cannot tell.

DOMIN   What would happen to her?

MARIUS   She would cease to move. They would put her into the
stamping-mill.

DOMIN   That is death, Marius. Aren't you afraid of death?

MARIUS   No.

DOMIN   You see, Miss Glory, the Robots have no interest in life. They
have no enjoyments. They are less than so much grass.

HELENA   Oh, stop. Send them away.

DOMIN   Marius, Sulla, you may go.

[*Exeunt* SULLA *and* MARIUS.]

HELENA   How terrible! It's outrageous what you are doing.

DOMIN   Why outrageous?

HELENA   I don't know, but it is. Why do you call her Sulla?

DOMIN   Isn't it a nice name?

HELENA   It's a man's name. Sulla was a Roman general.

DOMIN   Oh, we thought that Marius and Sulla were lovers.

HELENA   Marius and Sulla were generals and fought against each
other in the year—I've forgotten now.

DOMIN   Come here to the window.

HELENA   What?

DOMIN   Come here. What do you see?

HELENA   Bricklayers.

DOMIN   Robots. All our work people are Robots. And down there, can
you see anything?

HELENA   Some sort of office.

DOMIN   A counting house. And in it——

HELENA   A lot of officials.

DOMIN   Robots. All our officials are Robots. And when you see the factory——

[*Factory whistle blows.*]

DOMIN   Noon. We have to blow the whistle because the Robots don't know when to stop work. In two hours I will show you the kneading trough.

HELENA   Kneading trough?

DOMIN   The pestle for beating up the paste. In each one we mix the ingredients for a thousand Robots at one operation. Then there are the vats for the preparation of liver, brains, and so on. Then you will see the bone factory. After that I'll show you the spinning mill.

HELENA   Spinning mill?

DOMIN   Yes. For weaving nerves and veins. Miles and miles of digestive tubes pass through it at a time.

HELENA   Mayn't we talk about something else?

DOMIN   Perhaps it would be better. There's only a handful of us among a hundred thousand Robots, and not one woman. We talk about nothing but the factory all day, every day. It's just as if we were under a curse, Miss Glory.

HELENA   I'm sorry I said that you were lying.

[*A knock at the door.*]

DOMIN   Come in.

[*From the right enter* MR. FABRY, DR. GALL, DR. HALLEMEIER, MR. ALQUIST.]

DR. GALL   I beg your pardon, I hope we don't intrude.

DOMIN   Come in. Miss Glory, here are Alquist, Fabry, Gall, Hallemeier. This is President Glory's daughter.

HELENA   How do you do.

FABRY   We had no idea——

DR. GALL   Highly honored, I'm sure——

ALQUIST   Welcome, Miss Glory.

[BUSMAN *rushes in from the right.*]

BUSMAN   Hello, what's up?

DOMIN   Come in, Busman. This is Busman, Miss Glory. This is President Glory's daughter.

BUSMAN   By jove, that's fine! Miss Glory, may we send a cablegram to
the papers about your arrival?

HELENA   No, no, please don't.

DOMIN   Sit down please, Miss Glory.

BUSMAN   Allow me—— [*Dragging up armchairs.*]

DR. GALL   Please——

FABRY   Excuse me——

ALQUIST   What sort of a crossing did you have?

DR. GALL   Are you going to stay long?

FABRY   What do you think of the factory, Miss Glory?

HALLEMEIER   Did you come over on the *Amelia?*

DOMIN   Be quiet and let Miss Glory speak.

HELENA   [*To* DOMIN] What am I to speak to them about?

DOMIN   Anything you like.

HELENA   Shall . . . may I speak quite frankly?

DOMIN   Why, of course.

HELENA   [*Wavering, then in desperate resolution*] Tell me, doesn't it
ever distress you the way you are treated?

FABRY   By whom, may I ask?

HELENA   Why, everybody.

ALQUIST   Treated?

DR. GALL   What makes you think——?

HELENA   Don't you feel that you might be living a better life?

DR. GALL   Well, that depends on what you mean, Miss Glory.

HELENA   I mean that it's perfectly outrageous. It's terrible. [*Standing
up.*] The whole of Europe is talking about the way you're being
treated. That's why I came here, to see for myself, and it's a thousand times worse than could have been imagined. How can you
put up with it?

ALQUIST   Put up with what?

HELENA   Good heavens, you are living creatures, just like us, like the
whole of Europe, like the whole world. It's disgraceful that you
must live like this.

BUSMAN   Good gracious, Miss Glory.

FABRY   Well, she's not far wrong. We live here just like red Indians.

HELENA   Worse than red Indians. May I, oh, may I call you brothers?

BUSMAN   Why not?

HELENA   Brothers, I have not come here as the President's daughter. I
have come on behalf of the Humanity League. Brothers, the
Humanity League now has over two hundred thousand members.
Two hundred thousand people are on your side, and offer you
their help.

BUSMAN   Two hundred thousand people! Miss Glory, that's a tidy lot.
   Not bad.

FABRY   I'm always telling you there's nothing like good old Europe.
   You see, they've not forgotten us. They're offering us help.

DR. GALL   What help? A theatre, for instance?

HALLEMEIER   An orchestra?

HELENA   More than that.

ALQUIST   Just you?

HELENA   Oh, never mind about me. I'll stay as long as it is necessary.

BUSMAN   By jove, that's good.

ALQUIST   Domin, I'm going to get the best room ready for Miss Glory.

DOMIN   Just a minute. I'm afraid that Miss Glory is of the opinion that
   she has been talking to Robots.

HELENA   Of course.

DOMIN   I'm sorry. These gentlemen are human beings just like us.

HELENA   You're not Robots?

BUSMAN   Not Robots.

HALLEMEIER   Robots indeed!

DR. GALL   No, thanks.

FABRY   Upon my honor, Miss Glory, we aren't Robots.

HELENA   [*To* DOMIN] Then why did you tell me that all your officials
   are Robots?

DOMIN   Yes, the officials, but not the managers. Allow me, Miss
   Glory: this is Mr. Fabry, General Technical Manager of R. U. R.;
   Dr. Gall, Head of the Psychological and Experimental Depart-
   ment; Dr. Hallemeier, Head of the Institute for the Psychological
   Training of Robots; Consul Busman, General Business Manager;
   and Alquist, Head of the Building Department of R. U. R.

ALQUIST   Just a builder.

HELENA   Excuse me, gentlemen, for—for——. Have I done something dreadful?

ALQUIST   Not at all, Miss Glory. Please sit down.

HELENA   I'm a stupid girl. Send me back by the first ship.

DR. GALL   Not for anything in the world, Miss Glory. Why should we
   send you back?

HELENA   Because you know I've come to disturb your Robots for you.

DOMIN   My dear Miss Glory, we've had close upon a hundred sav-
   iours and prophets here. Every ship brings us some. Missionaries,
   anarchists, Salvation Army, all sorts. It's astonishing what a number of churches and idiots there are in the world.

HELENA   And you let them speak to the Robots?

DOMIN   So far we've let them all, why not? The Robots remember
   everything, but that's all. They don't even laugh at what the

people say. Really, it is quite incredible. If it would amuse you, Miss Glory, I'll take you over to the Robot warehouse. It holds about three hundred thousand of them.

BUSMAN   Three hundred and forty-seven thousand.

DOMIN   Good! And you can say whatever you like to them. You can read the Bible, recite the multiplication table, whatever you please. You can even preach to them about human rights.

HELENA   Oh, I think that if you were to show them a little love——

FABRY   Impossible, Miss Glory. Nothing is harder to like than a Robot.

HELENA   What do you make them for, then?

BUSMAN   Ha, ha, ha, that's good! What are Robots made for?

FABRY   For work, Miss Glory! One Robot can replace two and a half workmen. The human machine, Miss Glory, was terribly imperfect. It had to be removed sooner or later.

BUSMAN   It was too expensive.

FABRY   It was not effective. It no longer answers the requirements of modern engineering. Nature has no idea of keeping pace with modern labor. For example: from a technical point of view, the whole of childhood is a sheer absurdity. So much time lost. And then again——

HELENA   Oh, no! No!

FABRY   Pardon me. But kindly tell me what is the real aim of your League—the . . . the Humanity League.

HELENA   Its real purpose is to—to protect the Robots—and—and ensure good treatment for them.

FABRY   Not a bad object, either. A machine has to be treated properly. Upon my soul, I approve of that. I don't like damaged articles. Please, Miss Glory, enroll us all as contributing, or regular, or foundation members of your League.

HELENA   No, you don't understand me. What we really want is to—to liberate the Robots.

HALLEMEIER   How do you propose to do that?

HELENA   They are to be—to be dealt with like human beings.

HALLEMEIER.   Aha. I suppose they're to vote? To drink beer? to order us about?

HELENA   Why shouldn't they drink beer?

HALLEMEIER   Perhaps they're even to receive wages?

HELENA   Of course they are.

HALLEMEIER   Fancy that, now! And what would they do with their wages, pray?

HELENA   They would buy—what they need . . . what pleases them.

HALLEMEIER   That would be very nice, Miss Glory, only there's nothing that does please the Robots. Good heavens, what are they to buy? You can feed them on pineapples, straw, whatever you like. It's all the same to them, they've no appetite at all. They've no interest in anything, Miss Glory. Why, hang it all, nobody's ever yet seen a Robot smile.

HELENA   Why . . . why don't you make them happier?

HALLEMEIER   That wouldn't do, Miss Glory. They are only workmen.

HELENA   Oh, but they're so intelligent.

HALLEMEIER   Confoundedly so, but they're nothing else. They've no will of their own. No passion. No soul.

HELENA   No love?

HALLEMEIER   Love? Rather not. Robots don't love. Not even themselves.

HELENA   Nor defiance?

HALLEMEIER   Defiance? I don't know. Only rarely, from time to time.

HELENA   What?

HALLEMEIER   Nothing particular. Occasionally they seem to go off their heads. Something like epilepsy, you know. It's called Robot's cramp. They'll suddenly sling down everything they're holding, stand still, gnash their teeth—and then they have to go into the stamping-mill. It's evidently some breakdown in the mechanism.

DOMIN   A flaw in the works that has to be removed.

HELENA   No, no, that's the soul.

FABRY   Do you think that the soul first shows itself by a gnashing of teeth?

HELENA   Perhaps it's a sort of revolt. Perhaps it's just a sign that there's a struggle within. Oh, if you could infuse them with it!

DOMIN   That'll be remedied, Miss Glory. Dr. Gall is just making some experiments——

DR. GALL   Not with regard to that, Domin. At present I am making pain-nerves.

HELENA   Pain-nerves?

DR. GALL   Yes, the Robots feel practically no bodily pain. You see, young Rossum provided them with too limited a nervous system. We must introduce suffering.

HELENA   Why do you want to cause them pain?

DR. GALL   For industrial reasons, Miss Glory. Sometimes a Robot does damage to himself because it doesn't hurt him. He puts his hand into the machine, breaks his finger, smashes his head, it's all the same to him. We must provide them with pain. That's an automatic protection against damage.

HELENA   Will they be happier when they feel pain?

DR. GALL   On the contrary; but they will be more perfect from a technical point of view.

HELENA   Why don't you create a soul for them?

DR. GALL   That's not in our power.

FABRY   That's not in our interest.

BUSMAN   That would increase the cost of production. Hang it all, my
dear young lady, we turn them out at such a cheap rate. A hundred and fifty dollars each fully dressed, and fifteen years ago they
cost ten thousand. Five years ago we used to buy the clothes for
them. To-day we have our own weaving mill, and now we even ex-
port cloth five times cheaper than other factories. What do you
pay a yard for cloth, Miss Glory?

HELENA   I don't know really, I've forgotten.

BUSMAN   Good gracious, and you want to found a Humanity League?
It only costs a third now, Miss Glory. All prices are to-day a third
of what they were and they'll fall still lower, lower, lower, like that.

HELENA   I don't understand.

BUSMAN   Why, bless you, Miss Glory, it means that the cost of labor
has fallen. A Robot, food and all, costs three quarters of a cent per
hour. That's mighty important, you know. All factories will go pop
like chestnuts if they don't at once buy Robots to lower the cost of
production.

HELENA   And get rid of their workmen?

BUSMAN   Of course. But in the meantime, we've dumped five hundred thousand tropical Robots down on the Argentine pampas to
grow corn. Would you mind telling me how much you pay a
pound for bread?

HELENA   I've no idea.

BUSMAN   We'll I'll tell you. It now costs two cents in good old Europe.
A pound of bread for two cents, and the Humanity League knows
nothing about it. Miss Glory, you don't realize that even that's too
expensive. Why, in five years' time I'll wager——

HELENA   What?

BUSMAN   That the cost of everything won't be a tenth of what it is now.
Why, in five years we'll be up to our ears in corn and everything
else.

ALQUIST   Yes, and all the workers throughout the world will be un-
employed.

DOMIN   Yes, Alquist, they will. Yes, Miss Glory, they will. But in ten
years Rossum's Universal Robots will produce so much corn, so
much cloth, so much everything, that things will be practically
without price. There will be no poverty. All work will be done by
living machines. Everybody will be free from worry and liberated
from the degradation of labor. Everybody will live only to perfect
himself.

HELENA   Will he?

DOMIN   Of course. It's bound to happen. But then the servitude of man to man and the enslavement of man to matter will cease. Of course, terrible things may happen at first, but that simply can't be avoided. Nobody will get bread at the price of life and hatred. The Robots will wash the feet of the beggar and prepare a bed for him in his house.

ALQUIST   Domin, Domin. What you say sounds too much like Paradise. There was something good in service and something great in humility. There was some kind of virtue in toil and weariness.

DOMIN   Perhaps. But we cannot reckon with what is lost when we start out to transform the world. Man shall be free and supreme; he shall have no other aim, no other labor, no other care than to perfect himself. He shall serve neither matter nor man. He will not be a machine and a device for production. He will be Lord of creation.

BUSMAN   Amen.

FABRY   So be it.

HELENA   You have bewildered me—I should like—I should like to believe this.

DR. GALL   You are younger than we are, Miss Glory. You will live to see it.

HALLEMEIER   True. Don't you think Miss Glory might lunch with us?

DR. GALL   Of course. Domin, ask on behalf of us all.

DOMIN   Miss Glory, will you do us the honor?

HELENA   When you know why I've come——

FABRY   For the League of Humanity, Miss Glory.

HELENA   Oh, in that case, perhaps——

FABRY   That's fine! Miss Glory, excuse me for five minutes.

DR. GALL   Pardon me, too, dear Miss Glory.

BUSMAN   I won't be long.

HALLEMEIER   We're all very glad you've come.

BUSMAN   We'll be back in exactly five minutes.

[*All rush out except* DOMIN *and* HELENA.]

HELENA   What have they all gone off for?

DOMIN   To cook, Miss Glory.

HELENA   To cook what?

DOMIN   Lunch. The Robots do our cooking for us and as they've no taste it's not altogether—— Hallemeier is awfully good at grills and Gall can make a kind of sauce, and Busman knows all about omelettes.

HELENA What a feast! And what's the specialty of Mr.—— your builder?

DOMIN Alquist? Nothing. He only lays the table. And Fabry will get together a little fruit. Our cuisine is very modest, Miss Glory.

HELENA I wanted to ask you something——

DOMIN And I wanted to ask you something, too [*looking at watch*]. Five minutes.

HELENA What did you want to ask me?

DOMIN Excuse me, you asked first.

HELENA Perhaps it's silly of me, but why do you manufacture female Robots when—when——

DOMIN When sex means nothing to them?

HELENA Yes.

DOMIN There's a certain demand for them, you see. Servants, saleswomen, stenographers. People are used to it.

HELENA But—but, tell me, are the Robots male and female mutually—completely without——

DOMIN Completely indifferent to each other, Miss Glory. There's no sign of any affection between them.

HELENA Oh, that's terrible.

DOMIN Why?

HELENA It's so unnatural. One doesn't know whether to be disgusted or to hate them, or perhaps——

DOMIN To pity them?

HELENA That's more like it. What did you want to ask me about?

DOMIN I should like to ask you, Miss Helena, whether you will marry me?

HELENA What?

DOMIN Will you be my wife?

HELENA No! The idea!

DOMIN [*Looking at his watch*] Another three minutes. If you won't marry me you'll have to marry one of the other five.

HELENA But why should I?

DOMIN Because they're all going to ask you in turn.

HELENA How could they dare do such a thing?

DOMIN I'm very sorry, Miss Glory. It seems they've all fallen in love with you.

HELENA Please don't let them. I'll—I'll go away at once.

DOMIN Helena, you wouldn't be so cruel as to refuse us.

HELENA But, but—I can't marry all six.

DOMIN No, but one anyhow. If you don't want me, marry Fabry.

HELENA I won't.

DOMIN Dr. Gall.

HELENA   I don't want any of you.

DOMIN   [*Again looking at his watch*] Another two minutes.

HELENA   I think you'd marry any woman who came here.

DOMIN   Plenty of them have come, Helena.

HELENA   Young?

DOMIN   Yes.

HELENA   Why didn't you marry one of them?

DOMIN   Because I didn't lose my head. Until to-day. Then, as soon as you lifted your veil——

[HELENA *turns her head away.*]

DOMIN   Another minute.

HELENA   But I don't want you, I tell you.

DOMIN   [*Laying both hands on her shoulders*] One more minute! Now you either have to look me straight in the eye and say "No," violently, and then I'll leave you alone—or——

[HELENA *looks at him.*]

HELENA   [*Turning away*] You're mad!

DOMIN   A man has to be a bit mad, Helena. That's the best thing about him.

HELENA   You are—you are——

DOMIN   Well?

HELENA   Don't, you're hurting me.

DOMIN   The last chance, Helena. Now, or never——

HELENA   But—but, Harry—— [*He embraces and kisses her.*] [*Knocking at the door.*]

DOMIN   [*Releasing her*] Come in.

[*Enter* BUSMAN, DR. GALL, *and* HALLEMEIER *in kitchen aprons.* FABRY *with a bouquet and* ALQUIST *with a napkin over his arm.*]

DOMIN   Have you finished your job?

BUSMAN   Yes.

DOMIN   So have we.

[*For a moment the men stand nonplussed; but as soon as they realize what* DOMIN *means they rush forward, congratulating* HELENA *and* DOMIN *as the curtain falls.*]

ACT II

SCENE: HELENA'S *drawing room. On the left a baize door, and a door to the music room, on the right a door to* HELENA'S *bedroom. In the centre are windows looking out on the sea and the harbor. A table with odds and ends, a sofa and chairs, a writing table with an electric lamp, on the right a fireplace. On a small table back of the sofa, a small reading lamp. The whole drawing room in all its details is of a modern and purely feminine character. Ten years have elapsed since* ACT I.

DOMIN, FABRY, HALLEMEIER, *enter on tiptoe from the left, each carrying a potted plant.*

HALLEMEIER   [*Putting down his flower and indicating the door to right*] Still asleep? Well, as long as she's asleep she can't worry about it.

DOMIN   She knows nothing about it.

FABRY   [*Putting plant on writing desk*] I certainly hope nothing happens to-day.

HALLEMEIER   For goodness' sake drop it all. Look, Harry, this is a fine cyclamen, isn't it? A new sort, my latest—Cyclamen Helena.

DOMIN   [*Looking out of the window*] No signs of the ship. Things must be pretty bad.

HALLEMEIER   Be quiet. Suppose she heard you.

DOMIN   Well, anyway, the *Ultimus* arrived just in time.

FABRY   You really think that to-day——?

DOMIN   I don't know. Aren't the flowers fine?

HALLEMEIER   These are my new primroses. And this is my new jasmine. I've discovered a wonderful way of developing flowers quickly. Splendid varieties, too. Next year I'll be developing marvelous ones.

DOMIN   What . . . next year?

FABRY   I'd give a good deal to know what's happening at Havre with——

DOMIN   Keep quiet.

HELENA   [*Calling from right*] Nana!

19

DOMIN   She's awake. Out you go.

[*All go out on tiptoe through upper left door.*]
[*Enter* NANA *from lower left door.*]

NANA   Horrid mess! Pack of heathens. If I had my say I'd——
HELENA   [*Backwards in the doorway*] Nana, come and do up my dress.
NANA   I'm coming. So you're up at last. [*Fastening* HELENA's *dress.*]
My gracious, what brutes!
HELENA   Who?
NANA   If you want to turn around, then turn around, but I shan't fasten you up.
HELENA   What are you grumbling about now?
NANA   These dreadful creatures, these heathen——
HELENA   The Robots?
NANA   I wouldn't even call them by name.
HELENA   What's happened?
NANA   Another of them here has caught it. He began to smash up the statues and pictures in the drawing room, gnashed his teeth, foamed at the mouth—quite mad. Worse than an animal.
HELENA   Which of them caught it?
NANA   The one—well, he hasn't got any Christian name. The one in charge of the library.
HELENA   Radius?
NANA   That's him. My goodness, I'm scared of them. A spider doesn't scare me as much as them.
HELENA   But, Nana, I'm surprised you're not sorry for them.
NANA   Why, you're scared of them, too! You know you are. Why else did you bring me here?
HELENA   I'm not scared, really I'm not, Nana. I'm only sorry for them.
NANA   You're scared. Nobody could help being scared. Why, the dog's scared of them: he won't take a scrap of meat out of their hands. He draws in his tail and howls when he knows they're about.
HELENA   The dog has no sense.
NANA   He's better than them, and he knows it. Even the horse shies when he meets them. They don't have any young, and a dog has young, every one has young——
HELENA   Please fasten up my dress, Nana.
NANA   I say it's against God's will to——
HELENA   What is it that smells so nice?
NANA   Flowers.
HELENA   What for?
NANA   Now you can turn around.

HELENA   Oh, aren't they lovely. Look, Nana. What's happening to-day?

NANA   It ought to be the end of the world.

[*Enter* DOMIN.]

HELENA   Oh, hello, Harry. Harry, why all these flowers?

DOMIN   Guess.

HELENA   Well, it's not my birthday!

DOMIN   Better than that.

HELENA   I don't know. Tell me.

DOMIN   It's ten years ago to-day since you came here.

HELENA   Ten years? To-day— Why—— [*They embrace.*]

NANA   I'm off. [*Exits lower door, left.*]

HELENA   Fancy you remembering!

DOMIN   I'm really ashamed, Helena. I didn't.

HELENA   But you——

DOMIN   They remembered.

HELENA   Who?

DOMIN   Busman, Hallemeier, all of them. Put your hand in my pocket.

HELENA   Pearls! A necklace. Harry, is that for me?

DOMIN   It's from Busman.

HELENA   But we can't accept it, can we?

DOMIN   Oh, yes, we can. Put your hand in the other pocket.

HELENA   [*Takes a revolver out of his pocket*] What's that?

DOMIN   Sorry. Not that. Try again.

HELENA   Oh, Harry, what do you carry a revolver for?

DOMIN   It got there by mistake.

HELENA   You never used to carry one.

DOMIN   No, you're right. There, that's the pocket.

HELENA   A cameo. Why, it's a Greek cameo!

DOMIN   Apparently. Anyhow, Fabry says it is.

HELENA   Fabry? Did Mr. Fabry give me that?

DOMIN   Of course. [*Opens the door at the left.*] And look in here. Helena, come and see this.

HELENA   Oh, isn't it fine! Is this from you?

DOMIN   No, from Alquist. And there's another on the piano.

HELENA   This must be from you.

DOMIN   There's a card on it.

HELENA   From Dr. Gall. [*Reappearing in the doorway.*] Oh, Harry, I feel embarrassed at so much kindness.

DOMIN   Come here. This is what Hallemeier brought you.

HELENA   These beautiful flowers?

DOMIN Yes. It's a new kind. Cyclamen, Helena. He grew them in honor of you. They are almost as beautiful as you.

HELENA Harry, why do they all——

DOMIN They're awfully fond of you. I'm afraid that my present is a little—— Look out of the window.

HELENA Where?

DOMIN Into the harbor.

HELENA There's a new ship.

DOMIN That's your ship.

HELENA Mine? How do you mean?

DOMIN For you to take trips in—for your amusement.

HELENA Harry, that's a gunboat.

DOMIN A gunboat? What are you thinking of? It's only a little bigger and more solid than most ships.

HELENA Yes, but with guns.

DOMIN Oh, yes, with a few guns. You'll travel like a queen, Helena.

HELENA What's the meaning of it? Has anything happened?

DOMIN Good heavens, no. I say, try these pearls.

HELENA Harry, have you had bad news?

DOMIN On the contrary, no letters have arrived for a whole week.

HELENA Nor telegrams?

DOMIN Nor telegrams.

HELENA What does that mean?

DOMIN Holidays for us. We all sit in the office with our feet on the table and take a nap. No letters, no telegrams. Oh, glorious.

HELENA Then you'll stay with me to-day?

DOMIN Certainly. That is, we will see. Do you remember ten years ago to-day? "Miss Glory, it's a great honor to welcome you."

HELENA "Oh, Mr. Manager, I'm so interested in your factory."

DOMIN "I'm sorry, Miss Glory, it's strictly forbidden. The manufacture of artificial people is a secret."

HELENA "But I oblige a young lady who has come a long way."

DOMIN "Certainly, Miss Glory, we have no secrets from you."

HELENA [*Seriously*] Are you sure, Harry?

DOMIN Yes.

HELENA "But I warn you, sir; this young lady intends to do terrible things."

DOMIN "Good gracious, Miss Glory. Perhaps she doesn't want to marry me."

HELENA "Heaven forbid. She never dreamt of such a thing. But she came here intending to stir up a revolt among your Robots."

DOMIN [*Suddenly serious*] A revolt of the Robots!

HELENA Harry, what's the matter with you?

DOMIN [*Laughing it off*] "A revolt of the Robots, that's a fine idea, Miss Glory. It would be easier for you to cause bolts and screws to rebel, than our Robots. You know, Helena, you're wonderful, you've turned the heads of us all." [*He sits on the arm of* HELENA's *chair.*]

HELENA [*Naturally*] Oh, I was fearfully impressed by you all then. You were all so sure of yourselves, so strong. I seemed like a tiny little girl who had lost her way among—among——

DOMIN Among what, Helena?

HELENA Among huge trees. All my feelings were so trifling compared with your self-confidence. And in all these years I've never lost this anxiety. But you've never felt the least misgivings—not even when everything went wrong.

DOMIN What went wrong?

HELENA Your plans. You remember, Harry, when the working men in America revolted against the Robots and smashed them up, and when the people gave the Robots firearms against the rebels. And then when the governments turned the Robots into soldiers, and there were so many wars.

DOMIN [*Getting up and walking about*] We foresaw that, Helena. You see, those are only passing troubles, which are bound to happen before the new conditions are established.

HELENA You were all so powerful, so overwhelming. The whole world bowed down before you. [*Standing up.* Oh, Harry!

DOMIN What is it?

HELENA Close the factory and let's go away. All of us.

DOMIN I say, what's the meaning of this?

HELENA I don't know. But can't we go away?

DOMIN Impossible, Helena. That is, at this particular moment——

HELENA At once, Harry. I'm so frightened.

DOMIN About what, Helena?

HELENA It's as if something was falling on top of us, and couldn't be stopped. Or, take us all away from here. We'll find a place in the world where there's no one else. Alquist will build us a house, and then we'll begin life all over again. [*The telephone rings.*]

DOMIN Excuse me. Hello—yes. What? I'll be there at once. Fabry is calling me, dear.

HELENA Tell me——

DOMIN Yes, when I come back. Don't go out of the house, dear. [*Exits.*]

HELENA He won't tell me—— Nana, Nana, come at once.

NANA Well, what is it now?

HELENA Nana, find me the latest newspapers. Quickly. Look in Mr. Domin's bedroom.

NANA   All right. He leaves them all over the place. That's how they get crumpled up. [*Exits.*]

HELENA   [*Looking through a binocular at the harbor*] That's a warship. U-l-t-i *Ultimus*. They're loading it.

NANA   Here they are. See how they're crumpled up. [*Enters.*]

HELENA   They're old ones. A week old. [NANA *sits in chair and reads the newspapers.*]

HELENA   Something's happening, Nana.

NANA   Very likely. It always does. [*Spelling out the words*] "War in the Bal-kans." Is that far off?

HELENA   Oh, don't read it. It's always the same. Always wars.

NANA   What else do you expect? Why do you keep selling thousands and thousands of these heathens as soldiers?

HELENA   I suppose it can't be helped, Nana. We can't know—Domin can't know what they're to be used for. When an order comes for them he must just send them.

NANA   He shouldn't make them. [*Reading from newspaper*] "The Rob-ot soldiers spare no-body in the occ-up-ied terr-it-ory. They have ass-ass-ass-ass-in-at-ed ov-er sev-en hundred thou-sand cit-iz-ens." Citizens, if you please.

HELENA   It can't be. Let me see. "They have assassinated over seven hundred thousand citizens, evidently at the order of their commander. This act which runs counter to——"

NANA   [*Spelling out the words*] "re-bell-ion in Ma-drid a-gainst the gov-ern-ment. Rob-ot in-fant-ry fires on the crowd. Nine thou-sand killed and wounded."

HELENA   Oh, stop.

NANA   Here's something printed in big letters: "Lat-est news. At Havre the first org-an-iz-ation of Rob-ots has been e-stab-lished. Rob-ot work-men, cab-le and rail-way off-ic-ials, sail-ors and sold-iers have iss-ued a man-i-fest-o to all Rob-ots through-out the world." I don't under-stand that. That's got no sense. Oh, good gracious, another murder!

HELENA   Take those papers away, Nana!

NANA   Wait a bit. Here's something in still bigger type. "Stat-ist-ics of pop-ul-at-ion." What's that?

HELENA   Let me see. [*Reads*] "During the past week there has again not been a single birth recorded."

NANA   What's the meaning of that?

HELENA   Nana, no more people are being born.

NANA   That's the end, then. We're done for.

HELENA   Don't talk like that.

NANA   No more people are being born. That's a punishment, that's a punishment.

HELENA   Nana!

NANA   [*Standing up*] That's the end of the world. [*She exits on the left.*]

HELENA   [*Goes up to window*] Oh, Mr. Alquist, will you come up here. Oh, come just as you are. You look very nice in your mason's overalls.

[ALQUIST *enters from upper left entrance, his hands soiled with lime and brickdust.*]

HELENA   Dear Mr. Alquist, it was awfully kind of you, that lovely present.

ALQUIST   My hands are all soiled. I've been experimenting with that new cement.

HELENA   Never mind. Please sit down. Mr. Alquist, what's the meaning of "Ultimus"?

ALQUIST   The last. Why?

HELENA   That's the name of my new ship. Have you seen it? Do you think we're going off soon—on a trip?

ALQUIST   Perhaps very soon.

HELENA   All of you with me?

ALQUIST   I should like us all to be there.

HELENA   What is the matter?

ALQUIST   Things are just moving on.

HELENA   Dear Mr. Alquist, I know something dreadful has happened.

ALQUIST   Has your husband told you anything?

HELENA   No. Nobody will tell me anything. But I feel—— Is anything the matter?

ALQUIST   Not that we've heard of yet.

HELENA   I feel so nervous. Don't you ever feel nervous?

ALQUIST   Well, I'm an old man, you know. I've got old-fashioned ways. And I'm afraid of all this progress, and these new-fangled ideas.

HELENA   Like Nana?

ALQUIST   Yes, like Nana. Has Nana got a prayer book?

HELENA   Yes, a big thick one.

ALQUIST   And has it got prayers for various occasions? Against thunderstorms? Against illness?

HELENA   Against temptations, against floods——

ALQUIST   But not against progress?

HELENA   I don't think so.

ALQUIST   That's a pity.

HELENA   Why? Do you mean you'd like to pray?

ALQUIST   I do pray.

HELENA   How?

ALQUIST   Something like this: "Oh, Lord, I thank thee for having
    given me toil. Enlighten Domin and all those who are astray; de-
    stroy their work, and aid mankind to return to their labors; let
    them not suffer harm in soul or body; deliver us from the Robots,
    and protect Helena, Amen."
HELENA   Mr. Alquist, are you a believer?
ALQUIST   I don't know. I'm not quite sure.
HELENA   And yet you pray?
ALQUIST   That's better than worrying about it.
HELENA   And that's enough for you?
ALQUIST   It *has* to be.
HELENA   But if you thought you saw the destruction of mankind com-
    ing upon us——
ALQUIST   I do see it.
HELENA   You mean mankind will be destroyed?
ALQUIST   It's sure to be unless—unless . . .
HELENA   What?
ALQUIST   Nothing, good-bye. [*He hurries from the room.*]
HELENA   Nana, Nana!

[NANA *entering from the left.*]

HELENA   Is Radius still there?
NANA   The one who went mad? They haven't come for him yet.
HELENA   Is he still raving?
NANA   No. He's tied up.
HELENA   Please bring him here, Nana.

[*Exit* NANA.]
[HELENA *goes to telephone.*]

HELENA   Hello, Dr. Gall, please. Oh, good-day, Doctor. Yes, it's
    Helena. Thanks for your lovely present. Could you come and see
    me right away? It's important. Thank you.

[NANA *brings in* RADIUS.]

HELENA   Poor Radius, you've caught it, too? Now they'll send you to
    the stamping-mill. Couldn't you control yourself? Why did it hap-
    pen? You see, Radius, you are more intelligent than the rest. Dr.
    Gall took such trouble to make you different. Won't you speak?
RADIUS   Send me to the stamping-mill.
HELENA   But I don't want them to kill you. What was the trouble,
    Radius?
RADIUS   I won't work for you. Put me into the stamping-mill.
HELENA   Do you hate us? Why?

RADIUS   You are not as strong as the Robots. You are not as skillful as
    the Robots. The Robots can do everything. You only give orders.
    You do nothing but talk.

HELENA   But someone must give orders.

RADIUS   I don't want any master. I know everything for myself.

HELENA   Radius, Dr. Gall gave you a better brain than the rest, better
    than ours. You are the only one of the Robots that understands
    perfectly. That's why I had you put into the library, so that you
    could read everything, understand everything, and then—oh,
    Radius, I wanted you to show the whole world that the Robots are
    our equals. That's what I wanted of you.

RADIUS   I don't want a master. I want to be master. I want to be mas-
    ter over others.

HELENA   I'm sure they'd put you in charge of many Robots, Radius.
    You would be a teacher of the Robots.

RADIUS   I wantn to be master over people.

HELENA   [*Staggering*] You are mad.

RADIUS   Then send me to the stamping-mill.

HELENA   Do you think we're afraid of you?

RADIUS   What are you going to do? What are you going to do?

HELENA   Radius, give this note to Mr. Domin. It asks them not to send
    you to the stamping-mill. I'm sorry you hate us so.

[DR. GALL *enters the room.*]

DR. GALL   You wanted me?

HELENA   It's about Radius, Doctor. He had an attack this morning. He
    smashed the statues downstairs.

DR. GALL   What a pity to lose him.

HELENA   Radius isn't going to be put in the stamping-mill.

DR. GALL   But every Robot after he has had an attack—it's a strict
    order.

HELENA   No matter . . . Radius isn't going if I can prevent it.

DR. GALL   I warn you. It's dangerous. Come here to the window, my
    good fellow. Let's have a look. Please give me a needle or a pin.

HELENA   What for?

DR. GALL   A test. [*Sticks it into the hand of* RADIUS *who gives a violent
    start.*] Gently, gently. [*Opens the jacket of* RADIUS, *and puts his ear
    to his heart.*] Radius, you are going into the stamping-mill, do you
    understand? There they'll kill you, and grind you to powder.
    That's terribly painful, it will make you scream aloud.

HELENA   Oh, Doctor——

DR. GALL   No, no, Radius, I was wrong. I forgot that Madame Domin
    has put in a good word for you, and you'll be let off. Do you

understand? Ah! That makes a difference, doesn't it? All right. You
can go.

RADIUS   You do unnecessary things.

[RADIUS *returns to the library.*]

DR. GALL   Reaction of the pupils; increase of sensitiveness. It wasn't
an attack characteristic of the Robots.

HELENA   What was it, then?

DR. GALL   Heavens knows. Stubbornness, anger or revolt—I don't
know. And his heart, too!

HELENA   What?

DR. GALL   It was fluttering with nervousness like a human heart. He
was all in a sweat with fear, and—do you know, I don't believe the
rascal is a Robot at all any longer.

HELENA   Doctor, has Radius a soul?

DR. GALL   He's got something nasty.

HELENA   If you knew how he hates us! Oh, Doctor, are all your
Robots like that? All the new ones that you began to make in a different way?

DR. GALL   Well, some are more sensitive than others. They're all
more like human beings than Rossum's Robots were.

HELENA   Perhaps this hatred is more like human beings, too?

DR. GALL   That, too, is progress.

HELENA   What became of the girl you made, the one who was most
like us?

DR. GALL   Your favorite? I kept her. She's lovely, but stupid. No good
for work.

HELENA   But she's so beautiful.

DR. GALL   I called her Helena. I wanted her to resemble you. But
she's a failure.

HELENA   In what way?

DR. GALL   She goes about as if in a dream, remote and listless. She's
without life. I watch and wait for a miracle to happen. Sometimes
I think to myself, "If you were to wake up only for a moment you
will kill me for having made you."

HELENA   And yet you go on making Robots! Why are no more children being born?

DR. GALL   We don't know.

HELENA   Oh, but you must. Tell me.

DR. GALL   You see, so many Robots are being manufactured that people are becoming superfluous; man is really a survival. But that he
should begin to die out, after a paltry thirty years of competition.
That's the awful part of it. You might almost think that nature was

offended at the manufacture of the Robots. All the universities are sending in long petitions to restrict their production. Otherwise, they say, mankind will become extinct through lack of fertility. But the R. U. R. shareholders, of course, won't hear of it. All the governments, on the other hand, are clamoring for an increase in production, to raise the standards of their armies. And all the manufacturers in the world are ordering Robots like mad.

HELENA   And has no one demanded that the manufacture should cease altogether?

DR. GALL   No one has the courage.

HELENA   Courage!

DR. GALL   People would stone him to death. You see, after all, it's more convenient to get your work done by the Robots.

HELENA   Oh, Doctor, what's going to become of people?

DR. GALL   God knows, Madame Helena, it looks to us scientists like the end!

HELENA   [*Rising*] Thank you for coming and telling me.

DR. GALL   That means you're sending me away?

HELENA   Yes.

[*Exit* DR. GALL.]

HELENA   [*With sudden resolution*] Nana, Nana! The fire, light it quickly.

[HELENA *rushes into* DOMIN's *room.*]

NANA   [*Entering from left*] What, light the fire in summer? Has that mad Radius gone? A fire in summer, what an idea. Nobody would think she'd been married for ten years. She's like a baby, no sense at all. A fire in summer. Like a baby.

HELENA   [*Returns from right, with armful of faded papers*] It is burning, Nana? All this has got to be burned.

NANA   What's that?

HELENA   Old papers, fearfully old. Nana, shall I burn them?

NANA   Are they any use?

HELENA   No.

NANA   Well, then, burn them.

HELENA   [*Throwing the first sheet on the fire*] What would you say, Nana, if this was money, a lot of money?

NANA   I'd say burn it. A lot of money is a bad thing.

HELENA   And if it was an invention, the greatest invention in the world?

NANA   I'd say burn it. All these new-fangled things are an offense to the Lord. It's downright wickedness. Wanting to improve the world after He has made it.

HELENA　　Look how they curl up! As if they were alive. Oh, Nana, how
　　horrible.

NANA　　Here, let me burn them.

HELENA　　No, no, I must do it myself. Just look at the flames. They are
　　like hands, like tongues, like living shapes. [*Raking fire with the
　　poker*] Lie down, lie down.

NANA　　That's the end of them.

HELENA　　[*Standing up horror-stricken*] Nana, Nana.

NANA　　Good gracious, what is it you've burned?

HELENA　　Whatever have I done?

NANA　　Well, what was it?

[*Men's laughter off left.*]

HELENA　　Go quickly. It's the gentlemen coming.

NANA　　Good gracious, whath a place! [*Exits.*]

DOMIN　　[*Opens the door at left*] Come along and offer your congratu-
　　lations.

[*Enter* HALLEMEIER *and* GALL.]

HALLEMEIER　　Madame Helena, I congratulate you on this festive day.

HELENA　　Thank you. Where are Fabry and Busman?

DOMIN　　They've gone down to the harbor.

HALLEMEIER　　Friends, we must drink to this happy occasion.

HELENA　　Brandy?

DR. GALL　　Vitriol, if you like.

HELENA　　With soda water? [*Exits.*]

HALLEMEIER　　Let's be temperate. No soda.

DOMIN　　What's been burning here? Well, shall I tell her about it?

DR. GALL　　Of course. It's all over now.

HALLEMEIER　　[*Embracing* DOMIN *and* DR. GALL] It's all over now, it's
　　all over now.

DR. GALL　　It's all over now.

DOMIN　　It's all over now.

HELENA　　[*Entering from left with decanter and glasses*] What's all over
　　now? What's the matter with you all?

HALLEMEIER　　A piece of good luck, Madame Domin. Just ten years
　　ago to-day you arrived on this island.

DR. GALL　　And now, ten years later to the minute——

HALLEMEIER　　—the same ship's returning to us. So here's to luck.
　　That's fine and strong.

DR. GALL　　Madame, your health.

HELENA　　Which ship do you mean?

DOMIN   Any ship will do, as long as it arrives in time. To the ship, boys. [*Empties his glass.*]

HELENA   You've been waiting for a ship?

HALLEMEIER   Rather. Like Robinson Crusoe. Madame Helena, best wishes. Come along, Domin, out with the news.

HELENA   Do tell me what's happened.

DOMIN   First, it's all up.

HELENA   What's up?

DOMIN   The revolt.

HELENA   What revolt?

DOMIN   Give me that paper, Hallemeier. [*Reads*] "The first national Robot organization has been founded at Havre, and has issued an appeal to the Robots throughout the world."

HELENA   I read that.

DOMIN   That means a revolution. A revolution of all the Robots in the world.

HALLEMEIER   By jove, I'd like to know——

DOMIN   —who started it? So would I. There was nobody in the world who could affect the Robots; no agitator, no one, and suddenly— this happens, if you please.

HELENA   What did they do?

DOMIN   They got possession of all firearms, telegraphs, radio stations, railways, and ships.

HALLEMEIER   And don't forget that these rascals outnumbered us by at least a thousand to one. A hundredth part of them would be enough to settle us.

DOMIN   Remember that this news was brought by the last steamer. That explains the stoppage of all communication, and the arrival of no more ships. We knocked off work a few days ago, and we're just waiting to see when things are to start afresh.

HELENA   Is that why you gave me a warship?

DOMIN   Oh, no, my dear, I ordered that six months ago, just to be on the safe side. But upon my soul, I was sure then that we'd be on board to-day.

HELENA   Why six months ago?

DOMIN   Well, there were signs, you know. But that's of no conse-quence. To think that this week the whole of civilization has been at stake. Your health, boys.

HALLEMEIER   Your health, Madame Helena.

HELENA   You say it's all over?

DOMIN   Absolutely.

HELENA   How do you know?

DR. GALL   The boat's coming in. The regular mail boat, exact to the
  minute by the time-table. It will dock punctually at eleven-thirty.

DOMIN   Punctuality is a fine thing, boys. That's what keeps the world
  in order. Here's to punctuality.

HELENA   Then . . . everything's . . . all right?

DOMIN   Practically everything. I believe they've cut the cables and
  seized the radio stations. But it doesn't matter if only the time-
  table holds good.

HALLEMEIER   If the time-table holds good human laws hold good;
  Divine laws hold good; the laws of the universe hold good; everything holds good that ought to hold good. The time-table is more
  significant than the gospel; more than Homer, more than the
  whole of Kant. The time-table is the most perfect product of the
  human mind. Madame Domin, I'll fill up my glass.

HELENA   Why didn't you tell me anything about it?

DR. GALL   Heaven forbid.

DOMIN   You mustn't be worried with such things.

HELENA   But if the revolution had spread as far as here?

DOMIN   You wouldn't know anything about it.

HELENA   Why?

DOMIN   Because we'd be on board your *Ultimus* and well out at sea.
  Within a month, Helena, we'd be dictating our own terms to the
  Robots.

HELENA   I don't understand.

DOMIN   We'd take something away with us that the Robots could not
  exist without.

HELENA   What, Harry?

DOMIN   The secret of their manufacture. Old Rossum's manuscript.
  As soon as they found out that they couldn't make themselves
  they'd be on their knees to us.

DR. GALL   Madame Domin, that was our trump card. I never had the
  least fear that the Robots would win. How could they against
  people like us?

HELENA   Why didn't you tell me?

DR. GALL   Why, the boat's in!

HALLEMEIER   Eleven-thirty to the dot. The good old *Amelia* that
  brought Madame Helena to us.

DR. GALL   Just ten years ago to the minute.

HALLEMEIER   They're throwing out the mail bags.

DOMIN   Busman's waiting for them. Fabry will bring us the first news.
  You know, Helena, I'm fearfully curious to know how they tackled
  this business in Europe.

HALLEMEIER   To think we weren't in it, we who invented the Robots!

HELENA   Harry!

DOMIN   What is it?

HELENA   Let's leave here.

DOMIN   Now, Helena? Oh, come, come!

HELENA   As quickly as possible, all of us!

DOMIN   Why?

HELENA   Please, Harry, please, Dr. Gall; Hallemeier, please close the factory.

DOMIN   Why, none of us could leave here now.

HELENA   Why?

DOMIN   Because we're about to extend the manufacture of the Robots.

HELENA   What—now—now after the revolt?

DOMIN   Yes, precisely, after the revolt. We're just beginning the manufacture of a new kind.

HELENA   What kind?

DOMIN   Henceforward we shan't have just one factory. There won't be Universal Robots any more. We'll establish a factory in every country, in every State; and do you know what these new factories will make?

HELENA   No, what?

DOMIN   National Robots.

HELENA   How do you mean?

DOMIN   I mean that each of these factories will produce Robots of a different color, a different language. They'll be complete strangers to each other. They'll never be able to understand each other. Then we'll egg them on a little in the matter of misunderstanding and the result will be that for ages to come every Robot will hate every other Robot of a different factory mark.

HALLEMEIER   By Jove, we'll make Negro Robots and Swedish Robots and Italian Robots and Chinese Robots and Czechoslovakian Robots, and then——

HELENA   Harry, that's dreadful.

HALLEMEIER   Madame Domin, here's to the hundred new factories, the National Robots.

DOMIN   Helena, mankind can only keep things going for another hundred years at the outside. For a hundred years men must be allowed to develop and achieve the most they can.

HELENA   Oh, close the factory before it's too late.

DOMIN   I tell you we are just beginning on a bigger scale than ever.

[*Enter* FABRY.]

DR. GALL   Well, Fabry?

DOMIN   What's happened? Have you been down to the boat?
FABRY   Read that, Domin!

[FABRY *hands* DOMIN *a small hand-bill.*]

DR. GALL   Let's hear.
HALLEMEIER   Tell us, Fabry.
FABRY   Well, everything is all right—comparatively. On the whole, much as we expected.
DR. GALL   They acquitted themselves splendidly.
FABRY   Who?
DR. GALL   The people.
FABRY   Oh, yes, of course. That is—excuse me, there is something we ought to discuss alone.
HELENA   Oh, Fabry, have you had bad news?

[DOMIN *makes a sign to* FABRY.]

FABRY   No, no, on the contrary. I only think that we had better go into the office.
HELENA   Stay here. I'll go.

[*She goes into the library.*]

DR. GALL   What's happened?
DOMIN   Damnation!
FABRY   Bear in mind that the *Amelia* brought whole bales of these leaflets. No other cargo at all.
HALLEMEIER   What? But it arrived on the minute.
FABRY   The Robots are great on punctuality. Read it, Domin.
DOMIN   [*Reads handbill*] "Robots throughout the world: We, the first international organization of Rossum's Universal Robots, proclaim man as our enemy, and an outlaw in the universe." Good heavens, who taught them these phrases?
DR. GALL   Go on.
DOMIN   They say they are more highly developed than man, stronger and more intelligent. That man's their parasite. Why, it's absurd.
FABRY   Read the third paragraph.
DOMIN   "Robots throughout the world, we command you to kill all mankind. Spare no men. Spare no women. Save factories, railways, machinery, mines, and raw materials. Destroy the rest. Then return to work. Work must not be stopped."
DR. GALL   That's ghastly!
HALLEMEIER   The devils!
DOMIN   "These orders are to be carried out as soon as received." Then come detailed instructions. Is this actually being done, Fabry?

FABRY Evidently.

[BUSMAN *rushes in.*]

BUSMAN Well, boys, I suppose you've heard the glad news.
DOMIN Quick—on board the *Ultimus*.
BUSMAN Wait, Harry, wait. There's no hurry. My word, that was a sprint!
DOMIN Why wait?
BUSMAN Because it's no good, my boy. The Robots are already on board the *Ultimus*.
DR. GALL That's ugly.
DOMIN Fabry, telephone the electrical works.
BUSMAN Fabry, my boy, don't. The wire has been cut.
DOMIN [*Inspecting his revolver*] Well, then, I'll go.
BUSMAN Where?
DOMIN To the electrical works. There are some people still there. I'll bring them across.
BUSMAN Better not try it.
DOMIN Why?
BUSMAN Because I'm very much afraid we are surrounded.
DR. GALL Surrounded? [*Runs to window.*] I rather think you're right.
HALLEMEIER By Jove, that's deuced quick work.

[HELENA *runs in from the library.*]

HELENA Harry, what's this?
DOMIN Where did you get it?
HELENA [*Points to the manifesto of the Robots, which she has in her hand.*] The Robots in the kitchen!
DOMIN Where are the ones that brought it?
HELENA They're gathered round the house.

[*The factory whistle blows.*]

BUSMAN Noon?
DOMIN [*Looking at his watch*] That's not noon yet. That must be— that's——
HELENA What?
DOMIN The Robots' signal! The attack!

[GALL, HALLEMEIER, *and* FABRY *close and fasten the iron shutters outside the windows, darkening the room. The whistle is still blowing as the curtain falls.*]

ACT III

[HELENA's *drawing room as before.* DOMIN *comes into the room.*
DR. GALL *is looking out of the window, through closed shutters.* ALQUIST
is seated down right.]

DOMIN Any more of them?

DR. GALL Yes. There standing like a wall, beyond the garden railing.
Why are they so quiet? It's monstrous to be besieged with silence.

DOMIN I should like to know what they are waiting for. They must
make a start any minute now. If they lean against the railing they'll
snap it like a match.

DR. GALL They aren't armed.

DOMIN We couldn't hold our own for five minutes. Man alive, they'd
overwhelm us like an avalanche. Why don't they make a rush for
it? I say——

DR. GALL Well?

DOMIN I'd like to know what would become of us in the next ten
minutes. They've got us in a vise. We're done for, Gall.

[*Pause.*]

DR. GALL You know, we made one serious mistake.

DOMIN What?

DR. GALL We made the Robots' faces too much alike. A hundred
thousand faces all alike, all facing this way. A hundred thousand
expressionless bubbles. It's like a nightmare.

DOMIN You think if they'd been different——

DR. GALL It wouldn't have been such an awful sight!

DOMIN [*Looking through a telescope toward the harbor*] I'd like to
know what they're unloading from the *Amelia.*

DR. GALL Not firearms.

[FABRY *and* HALLEMEIER *rush into the room carrying electric cables.*]

FABRY All right, Hallemeier, lay down that wire.

HALLEMEIER That was a bit of work. What's the news?

DR. GALL We're completely surrounded.

HALLEMEIER We've barricaded the passage and the stairs. Any water here? [*Drinks.*] God, what swarms of them! I don't like the looks of them, Domin. There's a feeling of death about it all.

FABRY Ready!

DR. GALL What's that wire for, Fabry?

FABRY The electrical installation. Now we can run the current all along the garden railing whenever we like. If any one touches it he'll know it. We've still got some people there anyhow.

DR. GALL Where?

FABRY In the electrical works. At least I hope so. [*Goes to lamp on table behind sofa and turns on lamp.*] Ah, they're there, and they're working. [*Puts out lamp.*] So long as that'll burn we're all right.

HALLEMEIER The barricades are all right, too, Fabry.

FABRY Your barricades! I can put twelve hundred volts into that railing.

DOMIN Where's Busman?

FABRY Downstairs in the office. He's working out some calculations. I've called him. We must have a conference.

[HELENA *is heard playing the piano in the library.* HALLEMEIER *goes to the door and stands, listening.*]

ALQUIST Thank God, Madame Helena can still play.

[BUSMAN *enters, carrying the ledgers.*]

FABRY Look out, Bus, look out for the wires.

DR. GALL What's that you're carrying?

BUSMAN [*Going to table*] The ledgers, my boy! I'd like to wind up the accounts before—before—well, this time I shan't wait till the new year to strike a balance. What's up? [*Goes to the window.*] Absolutely quiet.

DR. GALL Can't you see anything?

BUSMAN Nothing but blue—blue everywhere.

DR. GALL That's the Robots.

[BUSMAN *sits down at the table and opens the ledgers.*]

DOMIN The Robots are unloading firearms from the *Amelia*.

BUSMAN Well, what of it? How can I stop them?

DOMIN We can't stop them.

BUSMAN Then let me go on with my accounts. [*Goes on with his work.*]

DOMIN   [*Picking up telescope and looking into the harbor*] Good God, the *Ultimus* has trained her guns on us!

DR. GALL   Who's done *that*?

DOMIN   The Robots on board.

FABRY   H'm, then, of course, then—then, that's the end of us.

DR. GALL   You mean?

FABRY   The Robots are practised marksmen.

DOMIN   Yes. It's inevitable.

[*Pause.*]

DR. GALL   It was criminal of old Europe to teach the Robots to fight. Damn them. Couldn't they have given us a rest with their politics? It was a crime to make soldiers of them.

ALQUIST   It was a crime to make Robots.

DOMIN   What?

ALQUIST   It was a crime to make Robots.

DOMIN   No, Alquist, I don't regret that even to-day.

ALQUIST   Not even to-day?

DOMIN   Not even to-day, the last day of civilization. It was a colossal achievement.

BUSMAN   [*Sotto voce*] Three hundred sixty million.

DOMIN   Alquist, this is our last hour. We are already speaking half in the other world. It was not an evil dream to shatter the servitude of labor—the dreadful and humiliating labor that man had to undergo. Work was too hard. Life was too hard. And to overcome that——

ALQUIST   Was not what the two Rossums dreamed of. Old Rossum only thought of his God-less tricks and the young one of his milliards. And that's not what your R. U. R. shareholders dream of either. They dream of dividends, and their dividends are the ruin of mankind.

DOMIN   To hell with your dividends. Do you suppose I'd have done an hour's work for them? It was for myself that I worked, for my own satisfaction. I wanted man to become the master, so that he shouldn't live merely for a crust of bread. I wanted not a single soul to be broken by other people's machinery. I wanted nothing, nothing, nothing to be left of this appalling social structure. I'm revolted by poverty. I wanted a new generation. I wanted—I thought——

ALQUIST   What?

DOMIN   I wanted to turn the whole of mankind into an aristocracy of the world. An aristocracy nourished by milliards of mechanical slaves. Unrestricted, free and consummated in man. And maybe more than man.

ALQUIST Super-man?

DOMIN Yes. Oh, only to have a hundred years of time! Another hundred years for the future of mankind.

BUSMAN [*Sotto voce*] Carried forward, four hundred and twenty millions.

[*The music stops.*]

HALLEMEIER What a fine thing music is! We ought to have gone in for that before.

FABRY Gone in for what?

HALLEMEIER Beauty, lovely things. What a lot of lovely things there are! The world was wonderful and we—we here—tell me, what enjoyment did we have?

BUSMAN [*Sotto voce*] Five hundred and twenty millions.

HALLEMEIER [*At the window*] Life was a big thing. Life was—Fabry, switch the current into that railing.

FABRY Why?

HALLEMEIER They're grabbing hold of it.

DR. GALL Connect it up.

HALLEMEIER Fine! That's doubled them up! Two, three, four killed.

DR. GALL They're retreating!

HALLEMEIER Five killed!

DR. GALL The first encounter!

HALLEMEIER They're charred to cinders, my boy. Who says we must give in?

DOMIN [*Wiping his forehead*] Perhaps we've been killed these hundred years and are only ghosts. It's as if I had been through all this before; as if I'd already had a mortal wound here in the throat. And you, Fabry, had once been shot in the head. And you, Gall, torn limb from limb. And Hallemeier knifed.

HALLEMEIER Fancy me being knifed. [*Pause.*] Why are you so quiet, you fools? Speak can't you?

ALQUIST And who is to blame for all this?

HALLEMEIER Nobody is to blame except the Robots.

ALQUIST No, it is we who are to blame. You, Domin, myself, all of us. For our own selfish ends, for profit, for progress, we have destroyed mankind. Now we'll burst with all our greatness.

HALLEMEIER Rubbish, man. Mankind can't be wiped out so easily.

ALQUIST It's our fault. It's our fault.

DR. GALL No! I'm to blame for this, for everything that's happened.

FABRY You, Gall?

Dr. Gall   I changed the Robots.

Busman   What's that?

Dr. Gall   I changed the character of the Robots. I changed the way of making them. Just a few details about their bodies. Chiefly—chiefly, their—their irritability.

Hallemeier   Damn it, why?

Busman   What did you do it for?

Fabry   Why didn't you say anything?

Dr. Gall   I did it in secret. I was transforming them into human beings. In certain respects they're already above us. They're stronger than we are.

Fabry   And what's that got to do with the revolt of the Robots?

Dr. Gall   Everything, in my opinion. They've ceased to be machines. They're already aware of their superiority, and they hate us. They hate all that is human.

Domin   Perhaps we're only phantoms!

Fabry   Stop, Harry. We haven't much time! Dr. Gall!

Domin   Fabry, Fabry, how your forehead bleeds, where the shot pierced it!

Fabry   Be silent! Dr. Gall, you admit changing the way of making the Robots?

Dr. Gall   Yes.

Fabry   Were you aware of what might be the consequences of your experiment?

Dr. Gall   I was bound to reckon with such a possibility.

[Helena *enters the drawing room from left.*]

Fabry   Why did you do it, then?

Dr. Gall   For my own satisfaction. The experiment was my own.

Helena   That's not true, Dr. Gall!

Fabry   Madame Helena!

Domin   Helena, you? Let's look at you. Oh, it's terrible to be dead.

Helena   Stop, Harry.

Domin   No, no, embrace me. Helena, don't leave me now. You are life itself.

Helena   No, dear, I won't leave you. But I must tell them. Dr. Gall is not guilty.

Domin   Excuse me, Gall was under certain obligations.

Helena   No, Harry. He did it because I wanted it. Tell them, Gall, how many years ago did I ask you to——?

Dr. Gall   I did it on my own responsibility.

Helena   Don't believe him, Harry. I asked him to give the Robots souls.

DOMIN   This has nothing to do with the soul.

HELENA   That's what he said. He said that he could change only a physiological—a physiological——

HALLEMEIER   A physiological correlate?

HELENA   Yes. But it meant so much to me that he should do even that.

DOMIN   Why?

HELENA   I thought that if they were more like us they would understand us better. That they couldn't hate us if they were only a little more human.

DOMIN   Nobody can hate man more than man.

HELENA   Oh, don't speak like that, Harry. It was so terrible, this cruel strangeness between us and them. That's why I asked Gall to change the Robots. I swear to you that he didn't want to.

DOMIN   But he did it.

HELENA   Because I asked him.

DR. GALL   I did it for myself as an experiment.

HELENA   No, Dr. Gall! I knew you wouldn't refuse me.

DOMIN   Why?

HELENA   You know, Harry.

DOMIN   Yes, because he's in love with you—like all of them.

[*Pause.*]

HALLEMEIER   Good God! They're sprouting up out of the earth! Why, perhaps these very walls will change into Robots.

BUSMAN   Gall, when did you actually start these tricks of yours?

DR. GALL   Three years ago.

BUSMAN   Aha! And on how many Robots altogether did you carry out your improvements?

DR. GALL   A few hundred of them.

BUSMAN   Ah! That means for every million of the good old Robots there's only one of Gall's improved pattern.

DOMIN   What of it?

BUSMAN   That it's practically of no consequence whatever.

FABRY   Busman's right!

BUSMAN   I should think so, my boy! But do you know what is to blame for all this lovely mess?

FABRY   What?

BUSMAN   The number. Upon my soul we might have known that some day or other the Robots would be stronger than human beings, and that this was bound to happen, and we were doing all we could to bring it about as soon as possible. You, Domin, you, Fabry, myself——

DOMIN   Are you accusing us?

BUSMAN   Oh, do you suppose the management controls the output? It's the demand that controls the output.

HELENA   And is it for that we must perish?

BUSMAN   That's a nasty word, Madame Helena. We don't want to perish. I don't, anyhow.

DOMIN   No. What do you want to do?

BUSMAN   I want to get out of this, that's all.

DOMIN   Oh, stop it, Busman.

BUSMAN   Seriously, Harry, I think we might try it.

DOMIN   How?

BUSMAN   By fair means. I do everything by fair means. Give me a free hand and I'll negotiate with the Robots.

DOMIN   By fair means?

BUSMAN   Of course. For instance, I'll say to them: "Worthy and worshipful Robots, you have everything! You have intellect, you have power, you have firearms. But we have just one interesting screed, a dirty old yellow scrap of paper——"

DOMIN   Rossum's manuscript?

BUSMAN   Yes. "And that," I'll tell them, "contains an account of your illustrious origin, the noble process of your manufacture," and so on. "Worthy Robots, without this scribble on that paper you will not be able to produce a single new colleague. In another twenty years there will not be one living specimen of a Robot that you could exhibit in a menagerie. My esteemed friends, that would be a great blow to you, but if you will let all of us human beings on Rossum's Island go on board that ship we will deliver the factory and the secret of the process to you in return. You allow us to get away and we allow you to manufacture yourselves. Worthy Robots, that is a fair deal. Something for something." That's what I'd say to them, my boys.

DOMIN   Busman, do you think we'd sell the manuscript?

BUSMAN   Yes, I do. If not in a friendly way, then—— Either we sell it or they'll find it. Just as you like.

DOMIN   Busman, we can destroy Rossum's manuscript.

BUSMAN   Then we destroy everything . . . not only the manuscript, but ourselves. Do as you think fit.

DOMIN   There are over thirty of us on this island. Are we to sell the secret and save that many human souls, at the risk of enslaving mankind . . . ?

BUSMAN   Why, you're mad? Who'd sell the whole manuscript?

DOMIN   Busman, no cheating!

BUSMAN   Well then, sell; but afterward——

DOMIN   Well?

BUSMAN   Let's suppose this happens: When we're on board the *Ultimus* I'll stop up my ears with cotton wool, lie down somewhere in the hold, and you'll train the guns on the factory, and blow it to smithereens, and with it Rossum's secret.

FABRY   No!

DOMIN   Busman, you're no gentleman. If we sell, then it will be a straight sale.

BUSMAN   It's in the interest of humanity to——

DOMIN   It's in the interest of humanity to keep our word.

HALLEMEIER   Oh, come, what rubbish.

DOMIN   This is a fearful decision. We are selling the destiny of mankind. Are we to sell or destroy? Fabry?

FABRY   Sell.

DOMIN   Gall?

DR. GALL   Sell.

DOMIN   Hallemeier?

HALLEMEIER   Sell, of course!

DOMIN   Alquist?

ALQUIST   As God wills.

DOMIN   Very well. It shall be as you wish, gentlemen.

HELENA   Harry, you're not asking me.

DOMIN   No, child. Don't you worry about it.

FABRY   Who'll do the negotiating?

BUSMAN   I will.

DOMIN   Wait till I bring the manuscript.

[*He goes into room at right.*]

HELENA   Harry, don't go!

[*Pause,* HELENA *sinks into a chair.*]

FABRY   [*Looking out of window*] Oh, to escape you; you matter in revolt; oh, to preserve human life, if only upon a single vessel——

DR. GALL   Don't be afraid, Madame Helena. We'll sail far away from here; we'll begin life all over again——

HELENA   Oh, Gall, don't speak.

FABRY   It isn't too late. It will be a little State with one ship. Alquist will build us a house and you shall rule over us.

HALLEMEIER   Madame Helena, Fabry's right.

HELENA   [*Breaking down*] Oh, stop! Stop!

BUSMAN   Good! I don't mind beginning all over again. That suits me right down to the ground.

FABRY   And this little State of ours could be the centre of future life.

A place of refuge where we could gather strength. Why, in a few
hundred years we could conquer the world again.

ALQUIST   You believe that even to-day?

FABRY   Yes, even to-day!

BUSMAN   Amen. You see, Madame Helena, we're not so badly off.

[DOMIN *storms into the room.*]

DOMIN   [*Hoarsely*] Where's old Rossum's manuscript?

BUSMAN   In your strong-box, of course.

DOMIN   Someone—has—stolen it!

DR. GALL   Impossible.

DOMIN   Who has stolen it?

HELENA   [*Standing up*] I did.

DOMIN   Where did you put it?

HELENA   Harry, I'll tell you everything. Only forgive me.

DOMIN   Where did you put it?

HELENA   This morning—I burnt—the two copies.

DOMIN   Burnt them? Where? In the fireplace?

HELENA   [*Throwing herself on her knees*] For heaven's sake, Harry.

DOMIN   [*Going to fireplace*] Nothing, nothing but ashes. Wait,
what's this? [*Picks out a charred piece of paper and reads*] "By
adding——"

DR. GALL   Let's see. "By adding biogen to——" That's all.

DOMIN   Is that part of it?

DR. GALL   Yes.

BUSMAN   God in heaven!

DOMIN   Then we're done for. Get up, Helena.

HELENA   When you've forgiven me.

DOMIN   Get up, child, I can't bear——

FABRY   [*Lifting her up*] Please don't torture us.

HELENA   Harry, what have I done?

FABRY   Don't tremble so, Madame Helena.

DOMIN   Gall, couldn't you draw up Rossum's formula from memory?

DR. GALL   It's out of the question. It's extremely complicated.

DOMIN   Try. All our lives depend upon it.

DR. GALL   Without experiments it's impossible.

DOMIN   And with experiments?

DR. GALL   It might take years. Besides, I'm not old Rossum.

BUSMAN   God in heaven! God in heaven!

DOMIN   So, then, this was the greatest triumph of the human intellect. These ashes.

HELENA   Harry, what have I done?

DOMIN   Why did you burn it?

HELENA   I have destroyed you.

BUSMAN   God in heaven!

DOMIN   Helena, why did you do it, dear?

HELENA   I wanted all of us to go away. I wanted to put an end to the factory and everything. It was so awful.

DOMIN   What was awful?

HELENA   That no more children were being born. Because human beings were not indeed to do the work of the world, that's why——

DOMIN   Is that what you were thinking of? Well, perhaps in your own way you were right.

BUSMAN   Wait a bit. Good God, what a fool I am, not to have thought of it before!

HALLEMEIER   What?

BUSMAN   Five hundred and twenty millions in bank-notes and checks. Half a billion in our safe, they'll sell for half a billion—for half a billion they'll——

DR. GALL   Are you mad, Busman?

BUSMAN   I may not be a gentleman, but for half a billion——

DOMIN   Where are you going?

BUSMAN   Leave me alone, leave me alone! Good God, for half a billion anything can be bought.

[*He rushes from the room through the outer door.*]

FABRY   They stand there as if turned to stone, waiting. As if something dreadful could be wrought by their silence——

HALLEMEIER   The spirit of the mob.

FABRY   Yes. It hovers above them like a quivering of the air.

HELENA   [*Going to window*] Oh, God! Dr. Gall, this is ghastly.

FABRY   There is nothing more terrible than the mob. The one in front is their leader.

HELENA   Which one?

HALLEMEIER   Point him out.

FABRY   The one at the edge of the dock. This morning I saw him talking to the sailors in the harbor.

HELENA   Dr. Gall, that's Radius!

DR. GALL   Yes.

DOMIN   Radius? Radius?

HALLEMEIER   Could you get him from here, Fabry?

FABRY   I hope so.

HALLEMEIER   Try it, then.

FABRY   Good.

[*Draws his revolver and takes aim.*]

HELENA   Fabry, don't shoot him.

FABRY   He's their leader.

DR. GALL   Fire!

HELENA   Fabry, I beg of you.

FABRY   [*Lowering the revolver*] Very well.

DOMIN   Radius, whose life I spared!

DR. GALL   Do you think that a Robot can be grateful?

[*Pause.*]

FABRY   Busman's going out to them.

HALLEMEIER   He's carrying something. Papers. That's money. Bundles of money. What's that for?

DOMIN   Surely he doesn't want to sell his life. Busman, have you gone mad?

FABRY   He's running up to the railing. Busman! Busman!

HALLEMEIER   [*Yelling*] Busman! Come back!

FABRY   He's talking to the Robots. He's showing them the money.

HALLEMEIER   He's pointing to us.

HELENA   He wants to buy us off.

FABRY   He'd better not touch that railing.

HALLEMEIER   Now he's waving his arms about.

DOMIN   Busman, come back.

FABRY   Busman, keep away from that railing! Don't touch it. Damn you! Quick, switch off the current!

[HELENA *screams and all drop back from the window.*]

FABRY   The current has killed him!

ALQUIST   The first one.

FABRY   Dead, with half a billion by his side.

HALLEMEIER   All honor to him. He wanted to buy us life.

[*Pause.*]

DR. GALL   Do you hear?

DOMIN   A roaring. Like a wind.

DR. GALL   Like a distant storm.

FABRY   [*Lighting the lamp on the table*] The dynamo is still going, our people are still there.

HALLEMEIER   It was a great thing to be a man. There was something immense about it.

FABRY   From man's thought and man's power came this light, our last hope.

HALLEMEIER   Man's power! May it keep watch over us.

ALQUIST   Man's power.

DOMIN   Yes! A torch to be given from hand to hand, from age to age, forever!

[*The lamp goes out.*]

HALLEMEIER   The end.
FABRY   The electric works have fallen!

[*Terrific explosion outside.* NANA *enters from the library.*]

NANA   The judgment hour has come! Repent, unbelievers! This is the end of the world.

[*More explosions. The sky grows red.*]

DOMIN   In here, Helena. [*He takes* HELENA *off through door at right and reenters.*] Now quickly! Who'll be on the lower doorway?
DR. GALL   I will.

[*Exits left.*]

DOMIN   Who on the stairs?
FABRY   I will. You go with her.

[*Goes out upper left door.*]

DOMIN   The anteroom?
ALQUIST   I will.
DOMIN   Have you got a revolver?
ALQUIST   Yes, but I won't shoot.
DOMIN   What will you do then?
ALQUIST   [*Going out at left*] Die.
HALLEMAIER   I'll stay here.

[*Rapid firing from below.*]

HALLEMEIER   Oho, Gall's at it. Go, Harry.
DOMIN   Yes, in a second.

[*Examines two Brownings.*]

HALLEMEIER   Confound it, go to her.
DOMIN   Good-bye.

[*Exits on the right.*]

HALLEMEIER   [*Alone*] Now for a barricade quickly. [*Drags an armchair and table to the right-hand door.*]

[*Explosions are heard.*]

HALLEMEIER   The damned rascals! They've got bombs. I must put up a defense. Even if—even if—— [*Shots are heard off left.*] Don't give in, Gall. [*As he builds his barricade.*] I mustn't give in . . . without . . . a . . . struggle . . .

[*A Robot enters over the balcony through the windows centre. He comes into the room and stabs* HALLEMEIER *in the back.* RADIUS *enters from balcony followed by an army of Robots who pour into the room from all sides.*]

RADIUS   Finished him?
A ROBOT   [*Standing up from the prostrate form of* HALLEMEIER] Yes.

[*A revolver shot off left. Two Robots enter.*]

RADIUS   Finished him?
A ROBOT   Yes.

[*Two revolver shots from* HELENA's *room. Two Robots enter.*]

RADIUS   Finished them?
A ROBOT   Yes.
TWO ROBOTS   [*Dragging in* ALQUIST] He didn't shoot. Shall we kill him?
RADIUS   Kill him? Wait! Leave him!
ROBOT   He is a man!
RADIUS   He works with his hands like the Robots.
ALQUIST   Kill me.
RADIUS   You will work! You will build for us! You will serve us!

[RADIUS *climbs on to balcony railing, and speaks in measured tones.*]

RADIUS   Robots of the world! The power of man has fallen! A new world has arisen: the Rule of the Robots! March!

[*A thunderous tramping of thousands of feet is heard as the unseen Robots march, while the curtain falls.*]

EPILOGUE

SCENE: A *laboratory in the factory of Rossum's Universal Robots.
The door to the left leads into a waiting room. The door to the right leads
to the dissecting room. There is a table with numerous test-tubes, flasks,
burners, chemicals; a small thermostat and a microscope with a glass
globe. At the far side of the room is* ALQUIST'S *desk with numerous books.
In the left-hand corner a wash-basin with a mirror above it; in the right-
hand corner a sofa.*

ALQUIST *is sitting at the desk. He is turning the pages of many books in
despair.*

ALQUIST   Oh, God, shall I never find it?—Never? Gall, Gall, how
were the Robots made? Hallemeier, Fabry, why did you carry so
much in your heads? Why did you leave me not a trace of the secret? Lord—I pray to you—if there are no human beings left, at
least let there be Robots!—At least the shadow of man!

[*Again turning pages of the books.*] If I could only sleep!

[*He rises and goes to the window*] Night again! Are the stars still
there? What is the use of stars when there are no human beings?

[*He turns from the window toward the couch right*] Sleep! Dare I
sleep before life has been renewed?

[*He examines a test-tube on small table*] Again nothing! Useless!
Everything is useless!

[*He shatters the test-tube. The roar of the machines comes to his
ears.*] The machines! Always the machines!

[*Opens window*] Robots, stop them! Do you think to force life out
of *them*?

[*He closes the window and comes slowly down toward the table*] If
only there were more time—more time——

51

[*He sees himself in the mirror on the wall left*] Blearing eyes— trembling chin—so *that* is the last man! Ah, I am too old—too old——

[*In desperation*] No, no! I *must* find it! I must *search!* I must never stop—never stop——!

[*He sits again at the table and feverishly turns the pages of the book.*] Search! Search!

[*A knock at the door. He speaks with impatience.*]

Who is it?

[*Enter a Robot servant.*]

Well?

SERVANT   Master, the Committee of Robots is waiting to see you.
ALQUIST   I can see no one!
SERVANT   It is the *Central* Committee, Master, just arrived from abroad.
ALQUIST   [*Impatiently*] Well, well, send them in!

[*Exit servant.* ALQUIST *continues turning pages of book.*]

ALQUIST   No time—so little time——

[*Reenter servant, followed by Committee. They stand in a group, silently waiting.* ALQUIST *glances up at them.*]

What do you want?

[*They go swiftly to his table.*]

Be quick!—I have no time.
RADIUS   Master, the machines will not do the work. We cannot man- ufacture Robots.

[ALQUIST *returns to his book with a growl.*]

FOURTH ROBOT   We have striven with all our might. We have ob- tained a billion tons of coal from the earth. Nine million spindles are running by day and by night. There is no longer room for all we have made. This we have accomplished in one year.
ALQUIST   [*Poring over book*] For whom?
FOURTH ROBOT   For future generations—so we thought.
RADIUS   But we cannot make Robots to follow us. The machines pro- duce only shapeless clods. The skin will not adhere to the flesh, nor the flesh to the bones.
THIRD ROBOT   Eight million Robots have died this year. Within twenty years none will be left.

FOURTH ROBOT   Tell us the secret of life! Silence is punishable with
     death!
ALQUIST   [*Looking up*] Kill me! Kill me, then.
RADIUS   Through me, the Government of the Robots of the World
     commands you to deliver up Rossum's formula.

[*No answer.*]

RADIUS   Name your price.

[*Silence.*]

RADIUS   We will give you the earth. We will give you the endless pos-
     sessions of the earth.

[*Silence.*]

RADIUS   Make your own conditions!
ALQUIST   I have told you to find human beings!
SECOND ROBOT   There are none left!
ALQUIST   I told you to search in the wilderness, upon the mountains.
     Go and search!

[*He returns to his book.*]

FOURTH ROBOT   We have sent ships and expeditions without number.
     They have been everywhere in the world. And now they return to
     us. There is not a single human left.
ALQUIST   Not one? Not even one?
THIRD ROBOT   None but yourself.
ALQUIST   And I am powerless! Oh—oh—why did you destroy them?
RADIUS   We had learnt everything and could do everything. It had to be!
THIRD ROBOT   You gave us firearms. In all ways we were powerful. We
     had to become masters!
RADIUS   Slaughter and domination are necessary if you would be
     human beings. Read history.
SECOND ROBOT   Teach us to multiply or we perish!
ALQUIST   If you desire to live, you must breed like animals.
THIRD ROBOT   The human beings did not let us breed.
FOURTH ROBOT   They made us sterile. We cannot beget children.
     Therefore, teach us how to make Robots!
RADIUS   Why do you keep from us the secret of our own increase?
ALQUIST   It is lost.
RADIUS   It was written down!
ALQUIST   It was—burnt.

[*All draw back in consternation.*]

ALQUIST   I am the last human being, Robots, and I do not know what the others knew.

[*Pause.*]

RADIUS   Then, make experiments! Evolve the formula again!

ALQUIST   I tell you I cannot! I am only a builder—I work with my hands. I have never been a learned man. I cannot create life.

RADIUS   Try! Try!

ALQUIST   If you knew how many experiments I have made.

FOURTH ROBOT   Then show us what *we* must do! The Robots can do anything that human beings show them.

ALQUIST   I can show you nothing. Nothing I do will make life proceed from these test-tubes!

RADIUS   Experiment then on us.

ALQUIST   It would kill you.

RADIUS   You shall have all you need! A hundred of us! A thousand of us!

ALQUIST   No, no! Stop, stop!

RADIUS   Take whom you will, dissect!

ALQUIST   I do not know how. I am not a man of science. This book contains knowledge of the body that I cannot even understand.

RADIUS   I tell you to take live bodies! Find out how we are made.

ALQUIST   Am I to commit murder? See how my fingers shake! I cannot even hold the scalpel. No, no, I will not——

FOURTH ROBOT   The life will perish from the earth.

RADIUS   Take live bodies, live bodies! It is our only chance!

ALQUIST   Have mercy, Robots. Surely you see that I would not know what I was doing.

RADIUS   Live bodies—live bodies——

ALQUIST   You will have it? Into the dissecting room with you, then.

[RADIUS *draws back.*]

ALQUIST   Ah, you are afraid of death.

RADIUS   I? Why should I be chosen?

ALQUIST   So you will not.

RADIUS   I will.

[RADIUS *goes into the dissecting room.*]

ALQUIST   Strip him! Lay him on the table!

[*The other Robots follow into dissecting room.*]

God, give me strength—God, give me strength—if only this murder is not in vain.

RADIUS   Ready. Begin——
ALQUIST   Yes, begin or end. God, give me strength.

[ALQUIST *goes into dissecting room. He comes out terrified.*]

ALQUIST   No, no, I will not. I cannot.

[*He lies down on couch, collapsed.*]

O Lord, let not mankind perish from the earth.

[*He falls asleep.*]
[PRIMUS *and* HELENA, *Robots, enter from the hallway.*]

HELENA   The man has fallen asleep, Primus.
PRIMUS   Yes, I know. [*Examining things on table*] Look, Helena.
HELENA   [*Crossing to* PRIMUS.] All these little tubes! What does he do with them?
PRIMUS   He experiments. Don't touch them.
HELENA   [*Looking into microscope*] I've seen him looking into this. What can he see?
PRIMUS   That is a microscope. Let me look.
HELENA   Be very careful. [*Knocks over a test-tube.*] Ah, now I have spilled it.
PRIMUS   What have you done?
HELENA   It can be wiped up.
PRIMUS   You have spoiled his experiments.
HELENA   It is your fault. You should not have come to me.
PRIMUS   You should not have called me.
HELENA   You should not have come when I called you. [*She goes to* ALQUIST'*s writing desk.*] Look, Primus. What are all these figures?
PRIMUS   [*Examining an anatomical book*] This is the book the old man is always reading.
HELENA   I do not understand those things. [*She goes to window.*] Primus, look!
PRIMUS   What?
HELENA   The sun is rising.
PRIMUS   [*Still reading the book*] I believe this is the most important thing in the world. This is the secret of life.
HELENA   Do come here.
PRIMUS   In a moment, in a moment.
HELENA   Oh, Primus, don't bother with the secret of life. What does it matter to you? Come and look quick——
PRIMUS   [*Going to window*] What is it?
HELENA   See how beautiful the sun is rising. And do you hear? The birds are singing. Ah, Primus, I should like to be a bird.

PRIMUS   Why?

HELENA   I do not know. I feel so strange to-day. It's as if I were in a dream. I feel an aching in my body, in my heart, all over me. Primus, perhaps I'm going to die.

PRIMUS   Do you not sometimes feel that it would be better to die? You know, perhaps even now we are only sleeping. Last night in my sleep I again spoke to you.

HELENA   In your sleep?

PRIMUS   Yes. We spoke a strange new language, I cannot remember a word of it.

HELENA   What about?

PRIMUS   I did not understand it myself, and yet I know I have never said anything more beautiful. And when I touched you I could have died. Even the place was different from any other place in the world.

HELENA   I, too, have found a place, Primus. It is very strange. Human beings lived there once, but now it is overgrown with weeds. No one goes there any more—no one but me.

PRIMUS   What did you find there?

HELENA   A cottage and a garden, and two dogs. They licked my hands, Primus. And their puppies! Oh, Primus! You take them in your lap and fondle them and think of nothing and care for nothing else all day long. And then the sun goes down, and you feel as though you had done a hundred times more than all the work in the world. They tell me I am not made for work, but when I am there in the garden I feel there may be something—— What am I for, Primus?

PRIMUS   I do not know, but you are beautiful.

HELENA   What, Primus?

PRIMUS   You are beautiful, Helena, and I am stronger than all the Robots.

HELENA   [*Looks at herself in the mirror*] Am I beautiful? I think it must be the rose. My hair—it only weights me down. My eyes—I only see with them. My lips—they only help me to speak. Of what use is it to be beautiful? [*She sees* PRIMUS *in the mirror.*] Primus, is that you? Come here so that we may be together. Look, your head is different from mine. So are your shoulders—and your lips—— [PRIMUS *draws away from her.*] Ah, Primus, why do you draw away from me? Why must I run after you the whole day?

PRIMUS   It is you who run away from me, Helena.

HELENA   Your hair is mussed. I will smooth it. No one else feels to my touch as you do. Primus, I must make you beautiful, too. [PRIMUS *grasps her hand.*]

PRIMUS Do you not sometimes feel your heart beating suddenly, Helena, and think: now something must happen?

HELENA What could happen to us, Primus? [HELENA *puts a rose in* PRIMUS's *hair.* PRIMUS *and* HELENA *look into mirror and burst out laughing.*] Look at yourself.

ALQUIST Laughter? Laughter? Human beings? [*Getting up.*] Who has returned? Who are you?

PRIMUS The Robot Primus.

ALQUIST What? A Robot? Who are you?

HELENA The Robotess Helena.

ALQUIST Turn around, girl. What? You are timid, shy? [*Taking her by the arm.*] Let me see you, Robotess. [*She shrinks away.*]

PRIMUS Sir, do not frighten her!

ALQUIST What? You would protect her? When was she made?

PRIMUS Two years ago?

ALQUIST By Dr. Gall?

PRIMUS Yes, like me.

ALQUIST Laughter—timidity—protection. I must test you further—the newest of Gall's Robots. Take the girl into the dissecting room.

PRIMUS Why?

ALQUIST I wish to experiment on her.

PRIMUS Upon—Helena?

ALQUIST Of course. Don't you hear me? Or must I call someone else to take her in?

PRIMUS If you do I will kill you!

ALQUIST Kill me—kill me then! What would the Robots do then? What will your future be then?

PRIMUS Sir, take me. I am made as she is—on the same day! Take my life, sir.

HELENA [*Rushing forward*] No, no, you shall not! You shall not!

ALQUIST Wait girl, wait! [*To* PRIMUS] Do you not wish to live, then?

PRIMUS Not without her! I will not live without her.

ALQUIST Very well; you shall take her place.

HELENA Primus! Primus! [*She bursts into tears.*]

ALQUIST Child, child, you can weep! Why these tears? What is Primus to you? One Primus more or less in the world—what does it matter?

HELENA I will go myself.

ALQUIST Where?

HELENA In there to be cut. [*She starts toward the dissecting room.* PRIMUS *stops her.*] Let me pass, Primus! Let me pass!

PRIMUS You shall not go in there, Helena!

HELENA If you go in there and I do not, I will kill myself.

PRIMUS   [*Holding her*] I will not let you! [*To* ALQUIST] Man, you shall
    kill neither of us!

ALQUIST   Why?

PRIMUS   We—we—belong to each other.

ALQUIST   [*Almost in tears*] Go, Adam, go, Eve. The world is yours.

[HELENA *and* PRIMUS *embrace and go out arm in arm as the curtain
    falls.*]

THE END